Not Just *Another* Story

Also by Jhimli Mukherjee Pandey

Non-fiction
A Gift of Goddess Lakshmi (with Manobi Bandopadhyay)

Translations
Kadambari Devi's Suicide Note (by Ranjan Bandyopadhyay)
Interrogation (by Sunil Gangopadhyay)
Nante Fante graphic novel series (by Narayan Debnath)
A Poetic Pilgrimage (by Satyam Roychowdhury)
The Ghost of Gosain Bagan (by Shirshendu Mukhopadhyay)

Not Just *Another* Story
a novel

jhimli mukherjee pandey

ALEPH

ALEPH BOOK COMPANY
An independent publishing firm
promoted by *Rupa Publications India*

First published in India in 2019
by Aleph Book Company
7/16 Ansari Road, Daryaganj
New Delhi 110 002

Copyright © Jhimli Mukherjee Pandey 2019

The author has asserted her moral rights.

All rights reserved.

This is a work of fiction. Names, characters,
places and incidents are either the product of the
author's imagination or are used fictitiously and any
resemblance to any actual persons, living or dead,
events or locales is entirely coincidental.

No part of this publication may be reproduced,
transmitted, or stored in a retrieval system, in any
form or by any means, without permission in writing
from Aleph Book Company.

ISBN: 978-93-88292-95-5

1 3 5 7 9 10 8 6 4 2

Printed and bound in India by Replika Press Pvt. Ltd.

This book is sold subject to the condition that it
shall not, by way of trade or otherwise, be lent,
resold, hired out, or otherwise circulated without the
publisher's prior consent in any form of binding or
cover other than that in which it is published.

To my twin flame...across the two worlds...

Prologue

As a reporter, you're used to reacting fast. It's a life of quick responses and short deadlines. And uncertainties abound. You're never bored, though. The excitement, the clock counting down, your pulse racing as you sprint to the finish line—these are the reasons I continue doing what I do even though it can get hard at times. But there are times when you feel like you've hit a wall and wondewr whether you should abandon the story. Will you actually prevail or come back empty-handed? At times you end up being lucky, much more than you ever expected. And these can be life-changing experiences.

We had just closed a celebratory edition of the paper—*Slumdog Millionaire* had swept the Oscars. *An Indian story*! That was the refrain. There was an air of jubilation in the office. Later that night, just as I was leaving for home, my editor in Delhi called to remind me that this was not the first such story. Many years ago, Kolkata had been in the spotlight when the BAFTAs had been announced. A documentary about Sonagachi, Kolkata's infamous red-light district, had won critical acclaim, dominating the headlines of the day. Gautam da, my editor, echoed what was already on my mind. I had been thinking of this documentary ever since the news of the huge win for *Slumdog* had started making the rounds. This was an opportunity for the Kolkata edition of the newspaper to steal the limelight with a breaking human interest story.

'We should do a follow-up piece on those kids,' Gautam da said with conviction.

The documentary, *Sex Citadel*, traced the lives of six children from Sonagachi as they navigated the new world of education. Sonagachi was not new to me. In fact, it was one of my beats and I had been filing offbeat human interest stories from there for over two decades. I had my sources in the red-light area; people who would call to give me information about the goings-on there and those I could call when I was following a story. But this time my mandate was not simple. What my editor wanted me to do was to track down the children who had been in the documentary and do a story on how their lives had changed after that award. I felt a pang of guilt—after having won acclaim for my story around the time of the award, I hadn't kept in touch with any of the people who were part of the documentary. All those young children would be adults now and it was unlikely they'd speak to me. Gautam da wanted an exclusive, especially with Lakshmi, the oldest of the children; she had stolen everyone's hearts.

'It's not going to be easy,' I tried to explain. I had, in fact, tried to track down Lakshmi some years back, but had got nowhere.

I knew Gautam da was already seeing the story in the paper.

'While the rest of the country is still reeling from the success of *Slumdog*, we can get a fresh angle for our paper,' his voice brimmed with excitement. I could imagine the veins on his forehead throbbing like they did when he got the scent of a good story.

I didn't respond with the same enthusiasm and Gautam da got impatient. 'You did that story earlier, why can't you go out there and track them down again?' he barked.

I didn't want to annoy him further, so I agreed. Gautam da had been like an elder brother to me and was my mentor. Even though he now headed all the newspaper's editions from Delhi, he was originally from Kolkata. He had taught me the basic tenets of journalism. Even today, he keeps an eye on my stories from Kolkata and carries some of them nationally. I knew he had praised me to his colleagues in Delhi. I couldn't let him down. Besides, it wasn't an unjustified demand. I had to try and track down the children.

A couple of days later, I found myself walking down one of the many ribbon-like lanes in the Sonagachi maze. With me was my photographer colleague, Sajal, still groggy from last night's party at the Press Club. My constant nervous chatter was getting to him. Gautam da had called at five that morning, bursting with excitement, as if the story was on his table and he was designing the page!

Now we were hurrying to meet my contact at Durjoy, an NGO that works with the sex workers of Sonagachi giving them information and assistance on health and legal issues. In case that didn't work, I would have to try talking to as many people as possible once the women started waking up. I was berating myself for having lost contact with the kids.

'You'll go crazy if you try to stay in touch with every person you've spoken to for a story over the last twenty-five years,' Sajal said calmly. But I was in no mood to listen to reason.

'I have to track her down,' I said stubbornly.

We negotiated piles of garbage, curled up sleeping dogs, a

maze of clotheslines, potholes and rows of parked cycle rickshaws as we made our way to Durjoy. This NGO has been the source of many of my stories for years. Several missionary societies and social groups in Kolkata and international groups had partnered with Durjoy, but its main overseas partner is the famous Hope for Life, a UK NGO. A regular train of foreign social workers and funds flow to Durjoy from the UK through the year.

The person in charge of Durjoy is Prateek, a young, energetic man, whose mother was a sex worker in Sonagachi. Today Prateek is the point of contact for any outsider trying to enter Sonagachi and I was no exception. But I had an edge over my competitors here. For years I have been trusted with secrets. I had never broken this trust, sometimes even at the cost of losing a sensational story. In times of trouble I have used my contacts at the Lalbazar city police headquarters to bail sex workers out of tricky situations. These had paid off in the past and I hoped against hope that they would pay off again.

Finally, we reached Durjoy at the end of Aswini Dutta Lane and I rang the doorbell. Prateek answered the door almost immediately.

'Come right in, ma'am. Come, sir!' he said.

'Sorry to bother you so early in the morning, Prateek, but you know how urgent it is today…' I entered the familiar office room and was grateful for the air-conditioned space. We'd endured the kilometre-long walk after we got off at the Sovabazar Metro Station under the unrelenting sun and humidity. Plonking my heavy bag on an empty chair I sat down and gestured to Sajal to do the same. Prateek had left the room and he came back with a bottle of cold water, two glasses, two steaming cups of tea and some biscuits on a tray. I felt grateful and smiled warmly at him.

Prateek poured two glasses of water and waited for me to catch my breath. He is always affable, something about him soothes and reassures. I began to hope. 'Thanks, Prateek. Any leads yet? Can you tell me where to find the two older kids?'

'Please have your tea. I told you, I will help as best as I can,' Prateek smiled.

'There you go,' Sajal said, picking a biscuit from the plate and sitting back in his chair.

I leaned forward. 'I got in touch with Raju and Kartick. They both live in the US and have agreed to talk to me later today.'

'That's right,' Prateek nodded, 'and Paresh and Phatik have moved to the UK and are completing their doctorate degrees. The other two still live in the city...'

'Great! Did you manage to contact them? Where are they? What do they do now?'

'Hold on, ma'am. It's not that simple. The two "children" are grown-up women today. Remember their names?'

'Of course. Lakshmi and Keka...' I had gone over my notes from that old story late last night.

'I asked Keka if she would meet you. She refused at first. She didn't want to remember that briefly hopeful time in her life. But I convinced her that hers was a powerful story.'

'Wonderful,' I said. 'Give me her phone number, Prateek.'

He read it out to me as I took it down. Then Prateek paused and seemed to be struggling with his decision. 'Lakshmi, the centre of everyone's attention at that time, is no more.'

'She's dead? But you said that two of them were still in the city?'

'Not dead,' Prateek said slowly as he stood up and walked to the window, 'but she's not Lakshmi any more… It's a long story and one that she should tell you herself. Since the documentary and the awards, she hasn't met anyone from the media and has always turned down my requests. You will be the first one to talk to her. She was very reluctant, but when I told her that you've been a friend to us and to the women of Sonagachi for over two decades, she agreed to see you. But I don't know if she'll agree to give you an interview and definitely no photographs. I've given her my word,' Prateek looked meaningfully at Sajal, who shrugged. 'This is the only way you can meet her.'

'She lives in Salt Lake City,' Prateek said, and paused as I looked up at him in surprise. Salt Lake City was a posh part of Kolkata. The city's bureaucrats, intellectuals and businessmen lived there. 'Also, she's called Anjali now.'

I got the strong feeling that there could be a bigger story here. So I agreed—no photographs and I would only print what she'd agree to, if she agreed at all.

Armed with the piece of paper on which Prateek had written down Anjali's address, I hailed a taxi and headed towards Salt Lake, waving goodbye to Sajal.

From Sonagachi, in the northern part of the city, to Salt Lake, which is in the east, was a long drive, negotiating rush-traffic hour snarls. When the taxi finally pulled up outside the house, I was stunned. It was a lavish three-storey stand-alone bungalow, beautifully designed, complete with a manicured front lawn. Salt Lake is a planned township where most of the houses are designed to stand out. High-rises are not permitted and the locality is dotted with beautiful bungalows. Before settling the taxi fare, I craned my neck out of the window to check that I had reached the right address. As the taxi left, I stood outside the ornate gate for a few moments before walking in. How did a girl born in Sonagachi end up here?

◆

A soft-spoken female housekeeper answered the door and led me into a quiet room. The plush furniture, tasteful artwork, a huge LED television paired with a home theatre and the mini bar in the cosiest corner of the room—all of it looked warm and inviting. Despite the heightened tension I felt as I waited for my hostess to make her appearance, the ambience had a soothing effect on me and I felt my taut nerves slowly relax. The housekeeper came back with a tall glass of chilled orange juice. I was thirsty and the condensation on the cold glass made me reach for it without thinking. The juice was freshly squeezed, not poured out of a tetra pack or can. I mentally thanked my hostess. As the cold juice hit my stomach, I shuddered and drew a deep breath that I hadn't realized I had been holding all morning.

'Hello! Sorry to have kept you waiting, ma'am,' said a soft musical voice that came from behind me. The girl who was walking towards me could easily pass for a model! She was tall, had a perfect hourglass figure, an aquiline nose and a small pretty mouth. Her large expressive eyes were her most attractive feature. She was dressed in a soft pink satin housecoat with a broad collar and wore matching bedroom slippers. She had to have been in her late twenties or early thirties according to my notes but she looked younger and more vibrant than I expected. I couldn't detect any make-up on her face. She came and sat down on the sofa opposite mine and placed her perfectly manicured hands in her lap. I couldn't make out the length of her hair, it was done up in a loose bun.

'Have you had breakfast, ma'am?' she asked.

I glanced at my watch. It was noon. Well past breakfast time. She caught my glance and smiled.

'I wake up around this time and have breakfast around noon. Brunch really… Old habits,' she smiled. 'Since I thought you might come by today, I woke up an hour early, but haven't eaten yet. Let's move to the dining table and chat there, if you don't mind.'

As we moved to the dining room, I quickly went over what I had for the story. Gautam da was not going to get what he had wanted, although I could file a short story with the information I already had by interviewing the other kids from the documentary. But this young woman intrigued me. I remembered her as a young girl in that documentary and I could not believe that this was the same person. One careless mistake on my part could put an end to this opportunity.

'I'll just have some more juice, Lakshmi…Anjali.' She didn't react to my tripping over her name. 'I've already had breakfast, so don't bother. I don't mind giving you company at the breakfast table,' I smiled.

Her meal was frugal. A slice of dry toasted brown bread, boiled egg whites, a cup of milk and a few pieces of ripe papaya. She poured two tall glasses of chilled juice from a tall jug and sat down to eat. I put my cell phone on silent, took a deep breath and prepared myself to listen to her. It would have been easier with a notepad and a pen. But I knew that a notepad can be a huge turn-off. And, in any case, this was going to be off the record, so I couldn't use any notes. But I had to listen carefully just in case I managed to change her mind.

For the next few minutes, the crackle of the crunchy toast that my hostess munched on and the butterflies in my stomach were all that I was aware of. Half an hour had passed since I stepped into the house. I yearned to get started but I allowed her the time she needed to start to trust me. I had to let her lead me through her story. The fact that she had allowed me into her home at all showed that she was ready to be a friend. But that was not enough.

'Ma'am, I hope you don't have a tape recorder or a hidden camera with you. I had repeatedly asked Prateek to tell you that. This is the first time since those heady days that I am facing a journalist. I have nothing to do with your world anymore, ma'am. I'm talking to you as a friend, not a reporter.' Her voice was soft but the tone quite firm. She was present and yet there was a sense of remoteness about her.

'I understand. I certainly have no tape recorder, or camera. I assured Prateek of that. When I write this report—' I broke off as she started to respond. '*If* I write this report, your identity will be completely protected,' I told her, convinced that I would be able to bring her around. Little did I know that I would not prevail.

'Ma'am, I like living in this locality because the people are not nosy; it gives me the anonymity I desire. The nameplate outside my door says Anjali Sinha, a completely made-up identity. Only a few people, like Prateek, know that. You know a part of my story, don't you?' she asked, looking up at me with her quiet, expressive eyes. The streak of sadness made them even more beautiful.

'Yes, I've known Prateek and his NGO for years and I've been working in Sonagachi for even longer. I interviewed you when the documentary won the award, you and the other children. I even did a phone interview with Paul Smith, the filmmaker as well as Father Julius. But I lost track of you afterwards. I knew that your mother did not allow you to emigrate to England with the Smith couple. But in recent years, every time I asked Prateek about you he would skirt the issue. He would just say that you had moved out of Sonagachi and that he had lost touch with you. But I didn't really believe him. When I called him last evening, I told him that after *Slumdog Millionaire* the spotlight is once again on the documentary and I would lose my job if I didn't manage to trace the kids in the film. I might have exaggerated a little...' I confessed.

She smiled.

'But my editor has actually slotted a follow-up to be carried in all the editions and it will be a huge loss of face if I am unable to come up with the report. So I kept nagging Prateek and at last he relented,' I summed up the purpose of my visit for Anjali.

By then Anjali had finished her meal and we rose from the dining table. She led me to the lounge area on the first floor of the house and ushered me to the divan that had a pretty Kashmiri throw on it. She insisted on arranging the cushions around me so that I could sit more comfortably. I had come here expecting to meet a vulnerable young woman, but she was the one putting me at ease. I looked around the room and expensive art objects looked back at me from every corner. It was a pleasure to be there. She did have good taste.

'You don't know how strongly Prateek advocated your cause, ma'am. He is quite in awe of you. He pleaded with me, saying that you are a friend of his NGO, and that you've helped him out in some tough situations. Initially I refused, but he wouldn't listen. He just kept on and on at me until I finally relented,' she said, sitting down at the other end of the divan, folding her feet under her.

'So where do you want me to start? From the very beginning?' she asked me.

A sly glance at my watch said that it was already past 1 p.m. But I had realized by now that there was no point worrying about my deadline. I didn't even want to check my mobile for the number of calls I had missed. Something told me that everything and everyone could wait.

'This, what I do, is a family trade,' she said with some scorn. 'My mother and grandmother were also in the business. And while my mother was a hard, difficult person, my grandmother was the one who showed me affection.'

'I don't think I ever met your grandmother,' I said.

'She died a few years before that documentary,' Anjali said sadly.

'You can't write about me, ma'am. It would mean the end of my livelihood. Would you still like to hear my story? And that of my mother and grandmother?'

'Absolutely,' I told her, fascinated by this matriarchal family and still very curious to know how Lakshmi/Anjali had got here.

It would take many meetings before I got the full story. And by that time, we had forged a close friendship and I never wrote her story. But I didn't regret that one bit.

BOOK I

1.

It was a hot and humid morning. Spring was nearing its end and summer was steadily marching in. For fourteen-year-old Sarajubala, it meant waking up even earlier so that she could complete her household chores. Being the eldest girl in the family, she had a lot to do at home before she could leave for the local pathshala with her brothers and sister. She was one of the few girls her age who still went to school. The rest of them were married and many of them had moved away. Some had even become mothers and Saraju heard about their weddings, pregnancies and babies when their mothers came over to chat with her mother in the afternoons.

Saraju shaded her eyes and looked up at the sky. It was 6.30 a.m. and the sun already felt sharp. As the day progressed, it would get more uncomfortable and sweaty. She tucked the loose end of her pallu into her waist, picked up the broom and started sweeping the courtyard.

'Saraju! Finally awake?' Bibha came out of the kitchen to talk to her daughter, alerted by the sound of the broom.

'I'm not late, Ma!'

'I don't understand how you can sleep till so late in the summer. Finish sweeping the courtyard and then call me. I have to lay out the grains to dry and you can pick the stones. I have soaked the clothes already, once you're done with the grains, we'll take the clothes to the pond and finish washing them. Okay?'

'Ma, last night you said that we had to finish de-husking the paddy on the dhenki first...'

'That has to be done as well. And don't forget that we will have to milk Lali.'

'Ma, why can't you ask Kamala kakima to help you? Do you think we'll be able to finish so much work in so little time? I have to go to the pathshala as well!'

'Kamala is already helping me in the kitchen. You don't worry about what others are doing or should do. Just hurry up and do what I tell you.'

Saraju was the oldest student at the Jamtala pathshala and stood out as she walked with her siblings, books and slate in hand. The stick-wielding master did not take much interest in teaching her, nor did she particularly enjoy school, but no one dared question Haripada's decisions, not even his wife. But it frustrated Bibha to see her daughter still at home when she should be taking care of her own husband and children. The other women of the village constantly taunted her. They thought Haripada was inviting ill fortune. Who would marry her at this age?

But Saraju, Haripada's eldest child, was also his favourite. So what if his firstborn was not a boy? Haripada would tell his wife that only the very lucky were blessed with a daughter as their firstborn. Daughters were messengers of Goddess Lakshmi and brought the family luck, he would say.

◆

Haripada had been the head of the family ever since his father had died a few years back. He had lost his mother many years ago. He was the eldest of five siblings—three brothers and two sisters. The sisters were married and lived in far-off places; the brothers and their families lived together.

The house was a simple one-storey structure on a raised platform; it had a tiled roof and mud walls. The kitchen was separated from the living area. A long veranda ran along the length of the house and rooms lined either side of it. There were six rooms—two for each brother and his family. From the veranda you could climb down the steps on to the spacious open courtyard that had mango, guava and coconut trees. At the corner of the courtyard was a well attached to a handpump. This water was used for drinking, washing and bathing. A little ahead, close to the fields, was the outdoor toilet. The family, while not affluent, was comfortable. There was enough rice in the granary, some vegetables in the fields, fish in the pond and cows to milk. What more did anyone want? Haripada was a satisfied man. All he wanted was a peaceful life, good health and education for his children.

A huge, shady jamun tree stood in the centre of the village. Perhaps it was from this tree that the village got its name—Jamtala. The cool shade of the ancient tree was quite naturally the meeting point for the villagers. Children played around it, older men sat with their hookahs under it, the village elders dozed in its shade on charpoys placed there. Though the majority of the population was Muslim, the Hindus lived just as comfortably in Jamtala, and the communities shared their food and rituals. The village had a mazhar where both Hindus and Muslims prayed. Both men and women would visit the pir of the mazhar with their problems. The Muslims participated in the annual charak fair that saw Hindu gajan sanyasis cross over from West Bengal and flock to Jamtala.

Most people were farmers here. After returning from their fields, they would invariably gather under the tree. The women would also sit in groups a little away from the menfolk, chat, mend torn clothes and linen or clean rice and pulses.

'Hari, you are too casual about your daughter. What is this school-going business, eh?' Haren kaka said, as he drew on the hookah.

'Kaka, it is best to educate your daughters, too. After all, an educated mother will raise educated children. Wasn't that what Tagore had said?'

'You and your city talk. Such lofty ideas don't suit us, they are meant for the babulok—moneyed people who live in the city. We are poor, simple people who have to marry off our daughters on time and teach our sons how to run the household.'

'Kaka, Saraju is fourteen... I know I have to look for a groom for her, but something tells me that the time is just not right to marry her off...I keep hearing about all the unrest in other parts of the country...' Haripada said haltingly. 'Let things settle down a bit...perhaps in a year,' his voice shook.

Haren kaka looked at Haripada and saw how emotional he had become. 'I mean it in the best way, Haripada. Get her married soon, you have other children to take care of as well.'

Haripada nodded and stretched out his hand and accepted the hookah from the older man, as if in agreement.

Later that night when Bibha entered the room and tried to raise the same topic, Haripada feigned sleep. These were troubled times, he couldn't hand Saraju over to just any suitor who came her way. What if he turned out to be wrong for her? But had he listened to the village elders and married off his oldest daughter, Saraju's story would have been an entirely different one.

Though Jamtala, a village in the Jessore District of East Pakistan, was a picture of peace, the country was about to go through one of its worst crises. West Pakistan was tightening its grip on its eastern flank. Though the Partition of 1947 had united East and West Pakistan, it was not destined to remain one country. The people of the East refused to accept Urdu as the official language because they felt that a foreign tongue was being imposed on them. Students in the universities fought alongside the intelligentsia to establish Bangla as the official language. After students of the Dhaka University were killed in 1952, there were widespread protests and years of civil unrest, forcing West Pakistan to allow official status to Bangla. But this remained an uneasy truce. Seeds of suspicion were sown on both sides and West Pakistan began to rule with an iron hand. The army was given unbridled power to unleash terror. Armed looting of villages, mass raping of women, maiming and kidnapping of children became routine. Several secret resistance groups mushroomed but most collapsed because the army had a huge network of spies. All suspicious activities were reported and wiped out with a heavy hand. Mutilated bodies of revolutionaries were often found hanging from trees in village squares as gruesome warnings.

Villages were torched and crops were destroyed to teach people what happened to those who dared to raise their heads. With every passing day, atrocities increased. This led to more and more people joining resistance groups, which ultimately gave birth to the Mukti Bahini. But there were hundreds of others who couldn't muster the courage to stay on. Leaving their homes behind, they crossed over to West Bengal. The year was 1968, and though the final offensive in the form of a war of liberation was still some time away, the protests had grown louder and more frequent.

Jamtala was located very close to the West Bengal border. During the 1947 Partition, this village did not see too much upheaval because of unmatched communal harmony. Some Hindu families who had relatives in Calcutta chose to sell their land and migrate, but the majority of the Hindu population stayed on, and tried their best to live as if nothing had changed. They pretended that the partition was just a political event they had heard about, something that had happened far from them. But this quiet was just a lull before the storm that started brewing, among many other places, from Jessore.

Plots were being hatched, sometimes in isolation and sometimes as part of a bigger conspiracy, in which volunteers from different villages participated. Bombs were made in secret holes to be hurled at the police and army men from West Pakistan in guerrilla operations. While East Pakistan's dream of liberation was now no secret, West Pakistan stepped up its vigil and terror. This story of freedom struggle was not different from many others. This one too was won on the bloody graves of thousands. While many laid down their lives in open conflict, there were many others whose lives were lost behind the scenes.

Hundreds of people were secretly getting ready to retaliate and joining forces with the Bangla national movement. On the surface, they worked, socialized and behaved as if nothing had changed, but in the dead of the night, they moved stealthily and silently, meeting leaders or sharing information. Haripada was one such agent.

Haripada kept his revolutionary activities concealed. The fact that he was soft-spoken and non-confrontational helped. While others discussed the political goings-on, the terror unleashed by the army and how Jamtala might not escape an armed attack, Haripada tried to look uninterested and did not participate too much in such conversations. But he regularly attended secret meetings in other villages and acted as a courier, carrying letters and arms. For two years he managed to avoid attention until one day, late in 1968.

The people of the village had noticed his secret meetings and disappearances. Soon many in the village knew what Haripada was up to. They reported everything to his brothers and demanded an explanation. Haripada's brothers threatened to report him to the authorities because they were under tremendous pressure from other villagers and because they feared for their own lives. Haripada had no choice but to run. He couldn't leave his family behind because he knew that the villagers and his brothers would sacrifice them to save their own lives.

The family sneaked out of the house and snaked their way out of the village, carrying what little they could. A bullock cart waited to take them out of Jessore, thanks to Haripada's revolutionary friends. They soon lost themselves among the hundreds of Hindu families who were crossing over to West Bengal for safety. On 7 December 1971, Jessore would become the first district of East Pakistan to be liberated from the Pakistan Army.

Haripada and his family reached the relief camp near Sealdah a week after they left home. After waiting with the other refugees in an open tent for a few days, Haripada and his family were allotted a shack. There were hundreds of families like them, tired, sore, fear writ large on their faces, unsure of what lay in store for them.

◆

Life changed completely for Saraju at the camp. No one asked her to study anymore. In fact, she hadn't seen her books since they left Jamtala. She hadn't had time to pack much when Haripada came home and told them that they had to flee at once.

In a matter of two weeks, Saraju seemed to have grown up. Bibha did not have to chide her to wake up early because she hardly slept for fear of the long queue outside the toilet every morning. She had never known hunger in her life, had always had clean clothes to wear and a proper roof over her head and comforts all around. At the camp, hunger pangs never seemed to leave her. Every day they would ladle out a handful of boiled rice floating in starch water and some mashed potatoes with chillies for lunch and dinner. On a good day, they got to eat khichdi and mixed vegetables. Back home Saraju had never imagined eating such food but here she would pray hard that the person serving would ladle a little extra onto her plate. No one complained. Not even her younger siblings. She hardly saw them make noise or fight each other like they used to at home.

Saraju missed her friends. She was old enough to realize that she would never see them again. That world was lost to her forever. She had no one to share these feelings with. Her mother seemed to be permanently annoyed. Her siblings were too young to understand her feelings. So Saraju kept to herself.

Haripada had not had any time to sell his property and had left Jamtala with some petty cash that evaporated even before they reached the Sealdah camp. He had no relatives in West Bengal, but had collected the addresses of some people that his revolutionary friends knew, people who had migrated to Kolkata during the partition in 1947. He didn't have the money to take a bus and go in search of these people. So he would set out on foot to explore, look for work and return hungry, tired and sore. On some lucky days, he would earn a few rupees from doing odd jobs.

Time changes everything and, after two months, even the squalor of the relief camp became tolerable and routine. The camp swarmed with children and, gradually, Saraju's siblings had company their own age.

Children are resilient, but Bibha couldn't accept her new living conditions and remained depressed. She stopped looking after the children and left that to Saraju. Bibha and the other women in the camp would sit outside their tents and recall their homes and the lives they had lost forever and worry about their children's futures. Sometimes they managed to laugh and joke and then, as if someone had nudged them hard with reality, they would fall silent.

Initially, Saraju's parents had been very scared of letting the children out of their sight. As they all got used to their surroundings and their neighbours, they relaxed. Haripada let down his guard as he developed a deep bond with the other men in the camp. Their shared misery, hunger and helplessness brought them closer. Soon, neither Haripada nor his wife seemed to mind when Saraju took her younger brothers and sisters to play with their other friends to the nearby clearing. They stayed away from home for longer stretches. Bibha was not the only mother who stopped fretting about her kids. The longer they stayed outside, the less they got underfoot.

Saraju slowly regained her vivacious nature and just like in Jamtala, she made quite a few friends here too. She grew particularly close to another girl her age, Lata, whose family had landed up at the camp from Khulna District. The two girls would often sit and chat as the younger children played in the clearing. Soon they were inseparable. Often when Bibha napped in the afternoon with the younger kids, Saraju would roam about the camp with Lata.

And then there was a retinue of hawkers who would come every afternoon with their colourful wares to entice all age groups. They came in not only with their goodies but also had tales to tell that sometimes seemed more attractive than the colourful trinkets and edibles in their glass boxes and iron trunks. While some sold cheap candies, dried mango strips, achaar and churan, there were others who were favourites with the older children, especially the girls, because of the coloured ribbons, hairpins, cheap bead necklaces and earrings that they sold. Saraju and her friends couldn't afford to buy anything but they enjoyed looking at the wares and chatting with the hawkers. One of the hawker, Ramen, was young and good-looking, and flirted with the girls of the camp. He told them many stories about life outside. The girls listened wide-eyed as he told them about the banks of the Hooghly, the Victoria Memorial, New Market and the lush green Maidan lined with trees.

'Would you believe that all this is within walking distance from here?' Ramen said one afternoon.

'The Maidan, for example, is less than half an hour away. We could sit under a tree and watch people play, have ice creams and just relax in the cool green expanse. Another day, I can take you to the mammoth Victoria Memorial.'

'We can't go that far, Ramen da. Our mothers will miss us,' Saraju said.

'Don't be silly…you both roam about the camp for hours every afternoon. Do they miss you then?'

'Umm…no. But how do you know so much about what we do?' Lata asked, wide eyed.

'How can a hot-blooded youth not know about young beauties like you two?' Ramen asked, grinning. The girls blushed and giggled.

'Okay, okay…no need to feel shy now. Thank your stars that you have found a dependable friend like me who can show you the world.'

Saraju and Lata were intrigued. They wanted to experience life outside.

Ramen told them that just a few hundred meters away from the camp, at a place called Moulali, foreigners gave away dresses, eatables and other trinkets to children and young boys and girls.

'Come with me and I will take you there. I know them well since I often take children to them. Don't worry at all. I will bring you back in an hour.'

At first, they didn't trust him, giggling and ignoring him every time he suggested it to them.

'Our mothers will beat us up if we leave the camp,' said Lata, the more outspoken of the two.

'No one will miss you if you slip out in the afternoon when the elders are sleeping,' Ramen told them. 'Come on, you're not scared little babies, are you?'

'You promise to bring us back to the camp in one hour?' the girls insisted.

'Listen, ladies, my word is like the Himalayas. Unshakeable.'

Ever since Ramen had told them about this foreigners' camp, it was all the two girls could talk about. They knew that their parents would never agree to them leaving the safety of the camp. If they got wind of their plan, it would mean the end of their freedom.

Saraju had often heard her father tell her mother to keep a close eye on her. As a young woman of marriageable age, he wanted to keep her close and safe. He frequently reminded Bibha that Saraju should be guarded as one guards one's jewellery. Bibha thought that her husband was rather late in being careful with Saraju. Had he been a little more practical, Saraju would have been married off long before disaster had struck.

The two girls knew well that the world outside the camp could be dangerous. But the thought of this adventure was so enticing that they had to take the chance. They carefully planned every detail so that they could successfully leave the camp and return without anyone noticing. Saraju was rather nervous but Lata pushed her.

'See, we've wanted to get out of this camp and explore the surroundings. Now we have an escort. Everyone knows him. Moreover, we now have a proper destination to go to instead of just roaming about aimlessly. Come on, we won't get another chance,' Lata said.

On Thursday when the vendor came at his usual time, the girls told him that they were prepared to go out with him. They made him promise that he would bring them back in an hour. He asked them to hang around the entrance of the camp at 3 p.m. That was the time when hardly anyone would be around—the women would be resting in the shade and the younger children would be taking their nap.

◆

'He's not there. Are we late? Did he come and leave already?' Saraju whispered. Her palms were cold and sweaty and her heart thudded hard. She looked around furtively. They had been waiting for nearly half an hour.

'But it's not 3 p.m. yet. I checked the clock in the community kitchen. He should be here any moment. He gave us his word. Let's wait a little longer,' Lata whispered back.

'Maybe we shouldn't wait, let's just go back to my tent,' Saraju said, clasping Lata's arm.

'Don't be stupid. If you behave oddly, people will spot us. Sit casually,' Lata said sternly.

Just then Ramen arrived, signalled to them and started walking. He was careful not to come into the camp so that the other children would not see him. The girls slipped out and followed. No one seemed to notice.

◆

Bibha shouted for her daughter, her voice a mixture of anger and disgust. She waited awhile, sure that her daughter was within earshot and would hurry back. When that didn't happen, Bibha popped her head out of the opening of the tent. It was getting dark, the sun had just set. What was the girl doing? It was their turn to wash the utensils at the community kitchen, but before that Saraju had to bring the clothes in. They had been left to dry on the clothesline in the afternoon.

Bibha had seen Saraju lying down with the other children when she had dozed off. The stifling heat at the camp in the afternoons had a soporific effect on her and she couldn't resist falling asleep. In fact, she was grateful for those hours of sleep; they made her forget the pain of being homeless and the despair of not knowing how to navigate their lives. When Bibha woke up Saraju wasn't in the tent. She must have gone to meet Lata. That girl! Getting older every day but still so immature!

Every day as the sun went down, she was reminded of her neat home in Jamtala with its tulsi bedi at the centre of the courtyard. The women of the household gathered there in the evenings, lit the lamps and blew the conch shells to ward off evil spirits and usher in Goddess Lakshmi. Bibha couldn't let go of that routine. After all, these were hard times and the gods needed to be appeased. So she lit the kerosene lantern, adjusted the flame, pulled the loose end of her sari over her head and sat down on the floor to pray. She teared up. Once she had finished her evening prayer, Bibha, still in a sour mood, started shaking her youngest, a boy of seven, who lay fast asleep.

'Wake up, you little rascal! Go out and look for your didi! Wake up, wake up!' The boy sat up rubbing his eyes.

'It's starting to get dark and this empress is still gallivanting outside without a care in the world. Go and fetch her immediately. Tell her how angry I am!' Bibha boxed the ears of her other son in frustration and he ducked.

Bibha decided to get the clothes herself. As she pulled the clothes off the line savagely, she muttered out aloud, 'Saraju! Badmayish meye! Where the hell are you?'

Bibha believed that clothes should not be left on the clothesline after dark because evil spirits would spread black magic on them as the gods had retired for the day.

When neither Saraju nor her other children returned, Bibha's anger subsided and she started to get worried. Yes, Saraju was irresponsible at times but she was never this late. Dumping the clothes on the cot, she went out to look for her children. When she finally found them, they were sitting together disconsolately near the entrance of the camp. Saraju was not with them. Bibha's heart dropped.

When they noticed her, the children started clamouring. 'We looked for Didi…'

'She's not here, Ma.'

'We can't find her.'

'No one has seen her.'

'Did you check the toilets? What about Lata's house?' Bibha's voice gave way.

♦

Saraju and Lata felt like they had been walking for hours. To start with, they had been too excited to notice that they had walked far away from the camp. The vendor had zigged and zagged through smaller lanes and the girls had lost their bearings completely.

'Please tell us how far we have to go. Our legs are aching!' Lata was the first to protest.

'Just a bit more. Come on, come on, this is going to be worth it!' Ramen said in a reassuring tone. 'You'll want to come here again and again and who knows when I'll feel like doing this kindness. I'm a busy man, you know.'

'But you said it was near, we've come so far away. They will soon miss us at home and raise an alarm! What if they find out we have come out of the camp?' Saraju whimpered.

'They will never find out,' the vendor laughed. There was

something in his tone that scared the girls.

'We don't want to go any farther. Please take us back!' Lata gripped Saraju's hand tightly. They stopped and refused to move.

'We don't want anything. We want to go back home,' Saraju joined in.

'Home? You call that hellhole your home? You girls deserve a better life!'

'We just want to go home. We want to go back to our parents,' Saraju whined.

Worried that the commotion might draw the attention of passers-by, the vendor came close to the girls and spoke in a low menacing tone.

'You better follow me quietly, or I will leave you here and go. You will have to find your way back all by yourself. Is that what you want to do?'

The girls were too scared to say anything and just held each other's hands. Almost in a trance they followed this man because going back to the camp on their own seemed impossible.

'Let's turn back and run,' Saraju hissed under her breath after a while.

'We'll lose our way, what if we get kidnapped' Lata balked. They still held hands as they walked behind Ramen, not willing to lose sight of him. He was their only hope.

'How do we know that this man is not a kidnapper himself?' Saraju asked.

'Oh, Saraju! He's not like that—we know him. Let us pray to Ma Kali instead.'

After what seemed like a never-ending walk, the girls reached a locality with narrow and dark lanes. Even the squalor of the refugee camp seemed nothing compared to what they saw here. The strangeness of the place, the odd looks on the faces of the women and their suggestive clothing horrified the two girls.

'Where have you brought us, Dada!' Lata whispered, fear choking her. Saraju started crying.

'Stop crying. We're almost there. You're going to start your new lives here.'

They stopped outside a rundown two-storey house. They entered through an opening—a gate had once stood there. There was a small patch of open space, green with moss and dank from the lack of sunlight and fresh air. A few broken bricks had been arranged as steps that led to tiny cubbyholes lined up on the ground floor. The man asked them to wait and went inside.

'Where are the foreigners? Lata, this place is scary! Let's go,' Saraju was shaking.

'Let's run. We'll go till the big road and then we can ask people the way back to the refugee camp,' Lata's voice was hoarse with fear.

But before they could move, Ramen came out, accompanied by a fat middle-aged woman. He strode forward, and grabbed both the girls in a tight grip. The woman now walked towards them, her arms akimbo.

'Ei chhuri gulo, don't make a sound! Don't you dare try to run!' her voice froze Saraju and Lata where they stood. Tears streamed down their cheeks and for some time all they did was look from the vendor to the woman and back in shock.

'We want to go home. Please ask him to take us back,' Lata pleaded with the woman.

'Kaan khule shune ne, you cannot go back. Toder aami kinechhi daam diye, bujhli? I have paid good money for you.

You're going to stay here and do what I tell you. Don't try any funny business or I'll take the skin off your back. Do as you're told and within a few days you'll learn to be happy.

'Ramen, now you go. I have paid you, no need to hang around here anymore,' she said, with a careless wave of her hand.

'Okay, Shefali didi. Now be good, you two,' Ramen turned around and started to walk away.

The girls fell at his feet and started wailing. Shefali pulled them away with the strength of a bull and Ramen escaped. Then she casually slapped them so hard their teeth rattled. Shefali pulled them up, dragged the malnourished girls like rag dolls into one of the dark rooms and pushed them in, and locked the door. By the time the girls overcame their shock and started to move, Shefali was long gone. 'Please, Didi, please have mercy on us and let us go…' Saraju pleaded. Lata kept banging on the door till her hands went numb.

'Oh, stop it, will you? Always the same with these new girls. See them a year from now and you'll not know them!' Shefali said, loud enough for everyone in the household to hear. Her heavy footsteps faded away.

Lata and Saraju were kept locked up in that dark and dingy room for days. Fear and shock had frozen the girls; they held on to each other, cried and fell asleep on the torn mat on the floor.

The door remained locked for most of the day. When they needed to visit the toilet, they would knock and Shefali would open the door, but the girls had to go one at a time. Two plates of rice, dal and sabji and a jug of water were also supplied to them twice a day. The girls were confused about what was happening. Their first thought was that they had landed up in a slave market. They were too naive to understand what a brothel was. Over the next few days, Shefali and the women who brought them their food tried to explain. Gradually, they learned that the place was called Sonagachi and it was a brothel where women earned their living by having sex with men.

Their captivity must have gone on for more than a week but the girls lost count of the number of days they had spent inside the room. Apart from the sliver of light that entered the dank room from below the door, they did not get to see the turn of the day. Since they spent most of the time whispering, crying and sleeping in exhaustion, they felt weak and unwell and their heads felt heavy and throbbed.

But whenever the two girls were awake, they made plans to escape.

'We'll knock on the door and ask to visit the toilet. When Shefali comes to open it, you step out and squint at the daylight outside to divert her attention. Then both of us will pounce on her, throw her to the ground and run,' Lata hatched a plan.

'She is so strong, Lata. Can we really overpower her? And what will she do to us if we get caught?'

'Don't be so timid. This is our only chance. We have to do it if we want to go home again,' Lata tried to sound confident.

'I'm with you, but I am so scared,' Saraju confessed.

'Okay, I used to observe the young men in the camp practise wrestling. I'll teach you some of the techniques. I'm sure we will be able to tackle Shefali,' Lata sounded confident.

A few days after the plan was hatched, Lata went for her bath and never came back. Saraju kept waiting for her friend. After almost an hour, she started banging on the door. When Shefali answered it, Saraju asked after Lata. She was told that Lata had been sold to her new owner. Saraju felt bereft.

2.

Saraju's solitary confinement without Lata seemed so unbearable that she would cry all day and refuse to eat. The walls of the room seemed to close in on her and choke her. Her wails could be heard all over the house. She would cry herself to sleep, wake up, remember what had happened and start crying again. The other girls in the household started feeling pity for her.

'Mashi, the new girl has stopped eating. Why don't you bring her out of that room and let her help us with the housework?' Kanan, the seniormost girl in Shefali's household, suggested to her. She had come to Shefali to hand over the agreed amount from her daily earnings at the end of the day.

'She's still fresh and might try to run. I don't have time to keep an eye on runaways,' Shefali said, irritated.

'Mashi, she will die like this. And even if she doesn't, you will have a living skeleton to sell if you don't let her out so that she can be among people,' Kanan spoke her mind and walked away.

'Huhh! Learn to speak with respect, you slip of a girl!' Shefali raised her voice, making sure Kanan heard her.

Shefali ruled her household of eight girls and three maids with a heavy hand. She didn't allow anyone to question her ways or volunteer suggestions.

'Pushpa, bring me tea! Where are you loafing? Don't you know it's my teatime?' Shefali barked.

She had sent Kanan off, but Shefali was also getting a little worried about her new girl. It had been a week since she had sold off Lata. She had known Saraju would take it hard. The girl's unending wails disturbed her. If she didn't eat she would indeed grow thin and her depression would tell on her looks. That would affect her price.

After having her tea, Shefali walked swiftly to Sonamukhi's house two lanes over. Sonamukhi, like Shefali, was a retired prostitute, one who had earned well during her prime, thanks to her long string of wealthy clients. She saved intelligently and bought her freedom from her owner. She had, using her connections with her long-time customers, bought a large house, which she successfully converted into a brothel. Shefali knew that Sonamukhi was on the lookout for a couple of new girls. She told her about Saraju.

The next day, Shefali took Saraju to Sonamukhi as planned. Sonamukhi felt pity for the frail Saraju, who hadn't bathed or eaten in days. She could tell that the girl came from a respectable background and with a little work could become a good earner. She sighed as she prepared to brighten her face to greet her new inductee.

'My, my, what a pretty face… How fair you are, my girl! But what a pity that you look so ill,' Sonamukhi said kindly, lifting Saraju's tear-stained face. 'Didn't they treat you well there?'

Saraju was startled at these kind words and broke down, covering her face with her hands. Shefali tried to speak up, to defend herself, but Sonamukhi signalled her to leave.

'Come, come, dear. Don't cry now. There's a good girl,'

Sonamukhi put her arm around Saraju.

When the girl finally stopped crying, Sonamukhi led her inside and made her sit beside her.

'Saraju, I understand that you were not prepared for this life. You are a good girl from a good family and dreamt of getting married one day and starting your own family. But destiny had a different plan for you and you have to accept it. I promise you, if you listen to me, I will take care of you,' Sonamukhi said.

'What work do you want me to do? I cannot cook that well but I can sweep and mop the floor, chop vegetables, wash clothes…' Saraju said, still unwilling to believe that she would have to have sex with strange men.

'Stupid girl! Why should you do all that? You will have maids to do all that for you. You just have to dress up and entertain. I'll teach you everything, don't worry.'

'I don't know how to sing and dance…'

'It's not just about singing and dancing. I'll get the other girls to explain it all to you. Now go up to your room and relax. Everything will fall into place.'

Sonamukhi was running out of patience and did not want to scold the new girl. She called some girls who were standing at a distance, observing Saraju and talking among themselves. 'Take her upstairs, get her bathed and let her rest for some time.'

The first few days in the new home were a blur. She followed instructions in a daze, eating, bathing, sleeping as she was told to do. She noticed that the other girls got dressed up and then took different men into the rooms and closed the door. She watched the women get ready every day. Some of the women tried to draw her into their banter, but she flinched and kept to herself.

By the end of the week, however, Sonamukhi had started

grooming the latest girl in her establishment. She could be kind, but there was a limit to her patience. After all, she was a very good businesswoman.

Saraju was cooperative enough when all she had to do was help the other girls get ready, try on new clothes, learn to dress herself. But when it came to learning the art of sex, she protested vehemently, still hoping that this was all a nightmare that would end. She was terrified at what was expected of her and loathed the goings-on in the household.

Back home in Jamtala, Saraju's friends would sometimes tease her about her own marriage, even though her father had wanted her to study. They would warn her not to be so tomboyish—climbing the mango tree or diving into the pond to swim or fishing with her male cousins. Her mother had tried to teach her the different ways to chop vegetables for the various curries that she would have to cook in her marital home. Marriage and men to her meant a dreamy world of unknown excitement, a bit scary but definitely not loathsome. But she had only a vague idea about what happened between a husband and wife behind closed doors in private.

Parvati, a young woman in Sonamukhi's establishment, was trying to teach Saraju what a customer would expect from her and how she should please him. Saraju didn't want to hear it—she had her hands over her ears as Parvati tried to explain what she had to do. Sonamukhi walked in and slapped Saraju hard across the face.

'Stop your nonsense, girl, or I will chain you up and throw you in a dark room like Shefali did. I try to be kind to you and this is how you thank me!' she looked terrifying and Saraju was stunned at this change in her. All this time, Sonamukhi had been kind to her and spoken to her sweetly.

It took them over a month to prepare Saraju for her first night. When the night finally came, Saraju was trembling. Parvati reminded her to breathe and smile. When the middle-aged man clumsily groped her breasts, moaned and grunted and suddenly ejaculated all over his clothes and hers, she thought that this had to be the worst of it. She closed her eyes tight and pretended she was sitting on the banks of the pond listening to the birds chirping all around her. But, of course, there was worse to come. The man was soon ready for the second round. No amount of thinking of the pond protected Saraju from the pain of losing her virginity to this clumsy man.

Saraju's virginity fetched Sonamukhi a hefty hundred rupees. The next morning when Sonamukhi gave Saraju her very first income of ten rupees, Saraju held on to it for so long that her fist became sweaty. When she finally opened her palm to iron out the note, she had steeled herself. Fate had played its game with her and she had to accept her new life. After all, what choice did she have?

She had to learn the ropes to survive and excel. Ever since she had stepped into Sonamukhi's household, Saraju never tried to run. In the first few weeks, she had seen how a girl who had run away from a nearby brothel had been brought back by the police. The local police worked in tandem with the brothel owners. Saraju got to hear about girls who were brought back and denied food for days till they grovelled and begged for mercy. Girls were generally not beaten up for fear of ugly bruises that would reduce their price. Even customers were warned that if they had left a mark on a girl, they would be charged extra.

When Saraju first came to Sonamukhi's household, she had been a terrified, crying mess. But slowly she developed a steely reserve that no one could penetrate. She was friendly with the other girls but held herself aloof. Soon she became Sonamukhi's favourite. Even though the other girls teased her about being a chamcha, they also respected her.

Sonamukhi noted with satisfaction that she had not made a mistake by taking in Saraju. The girl soon became an expert and the men came back for what she had to offer.

◆

It was late one night when Saraju knocked at Sonamukhi's door. The other girls were busy with their customers.

'Ke? Oh, is that you? Come in. What happened?' Sonamukhi was surprised to see Saraju at this time. She should have been with a client.

'Nothing, Amol babu just left and I have a short break. I wanted to see if you wanted me to press your feet.' Saraju had become Sonamukhi's favourite not only by being a good earner, but also by taking care of the older woman. She would bring her tea or nimbu paani, press her feet, make her paan and just sit and talk with her in a way that the other girls didn't.

But this time, Saraju had to have a difficult conversation with her Sona mashi, 'Mashi, I have to tell you something, but you have to promise not to get angry.'

Sonamukhi was instantly on her guard. She drew herself up and stared at Saraju, waiting.

'I am pregnant, Mashi…' Saraju whispered, staring at the floor.

'What?' Sonamukhi roared, drawing herself away from Saraju.

'Who?' she asked, since Saraju had been seeing only a few men regularly. 'Have you not been taking the pill? I thought you were a careful girl! No matter, get rid of it. I'll take you to the clinic tomorrow. Now get lost and let me catch my breath,' Sonamukhi waved Saraju away. Saraju did not move.

'I asked you to get lost!' Sonamukhi's temper was showing.

'Mashi, please let me keep the baby. Please, Mashi…I will work hard and make up for the loss,' Saraju said, tears flowing down her face.

'Keep the baby! Are you mad? How many months along are you?' Sonamukhi asked.

'I have missed my periods for two months now…'

Unlike other girls who would first discuss the matter amongst themselves, Saraju had not wasted any time in breaking the news to Sonamukhi. She had learned how complicated matters became when girls delayed abortion. Once the baby grew big, abortion pills didn't help and they had to go to quacks. Saraju had seen girls die of excessive bleeding and infection.

'So that's not too late. Let me see…' Sonamukhi tried to move aside the folds of Saraju's sari with a practiced hand to check her womb. Saraju quickly moved away.

'Don't behave like a novice, Saraju!' Sonamukhi scolded.

'Mashi, that might harm the baby. I want to keep the child.'

Sonamukhi was aghast. What was the girl saying? 'Impossible! Do you know what that means?' Sonamukhi sounded fierce but tried to keep her voice as low as she could. She had to be careful not to stir the household.

'Mashi, I have lost everything. I was born to good parents, had siblings and though I lost my home, I still had a family. I don't know where they are and what became of them. Perhaps they are not too far from where I am today. I remember that Sonagachi is walking distance from the refugee camp but I know

I can never go back to them. They will never accept me… If I have the child, I will once again have someone to call my own…my family…' Saraju said, wiping her eyes with the end of her pallu.

Sonamukhi stared at her in shock.

'I have never been disobedient with you and tried to cope with my circumstances here as best as I could, Mashi. If you allow me this one thing, I will remain your slave forever…' Saraju said. Then she sat there and wept till Sonamukhi got up and came and sat by her. They sat together almost like mother and daughter, silent in each other's grief.

'Do you know what it means to keep your child? You will be out of work for at least four months, maybe six. Will one of your babus provide for that? That's the only way you can keep it.'

Saraju knew now that she had some hope.

Eventually Sonamukhi allowed her to keep the child. Ratan babu did provide for her and the child when she stopped working from her ninth month till the baby was three months old. Saraju could work despite her pregnancy because all over the world, there were men with fetishes. And some of them enjoyed having sex with pregnant women and were even willing to pay a higher rate. Sonamukhi footed the rest of the expenses but kept track of them so Saraju could pay her back once she started working again. Thus, Saraju's only child, her daughter, Malati, was born into Sonamukhi's household.

◆

From the scared, naive young girl who first came into Sonamukhi's household, Saraju blossomed into a beauty and was soon one of the most sought after at Sonagachi. Her price escalated.

Malati became the darling of the household. Even Sonamukhi, who did not have great love for children and the mess that they brought with them, would often babysit her. The other girls took turns taking care of the baby whenever they were free. Malati never once wore a torn frock, always had slippers on her tiny feet and plenty to eat. Saraju didn't have to worry at all about her child, except to wonder if she was becoming a little spoilt.

When Malati was old enough, Saraju started teaching her the Bengali alphabet. She bought books and slate and chalk for her and encouraged her to learn.

'Bring your slate and chalk. I'll teach you how to write,' Saraju would tell Malati.

'No, no, Ma, I want to draw, not write.'

'Okay. Bring the charcoal then. Let's sit in the courtyard and draw on the floor.'

Sometimes, Saraju would cleverly start introducing the alphabet or the numbers with the drawings, till Malati caught on and started protesting.

'But if you don't learn, how will you read and write?' she asked her once.

'I don't want to read and write.'

'What do you want to do?'

'Play with dolls and dress up, like you do…' Malati would say.

At this Saraju became thoughtful. She didn't want Malati to enter the profession. She would have to marry her off fast and send her away from here. But how would she do that? Who would marry a prostitute's daughter? Perhaps a son of a fellow prostitute, but would he be able to provide for Malati? What if he pushes her into the business? A sigh escaped her as she looked at Malati, who had by then busied herself with her dolls.

Over the years, Saraju built her reputation with her customers while maintaining her friendships with the other women of the brothel and the neighbouring establishments. While the demand for younger girls was always high, some men appreciated the sophistication and care that Saraju was able to bring into the encounters—many of them stayed her customers for many years.

By the time Malati was ten years old, Saraju was able to buy her freedom from Sonamukhi's household. Sonamukhi had been upset and had cut Saraju off every time she tried to bring up the topic. But Saraju persisted and eventually Sonamukhi relented. Saraju had saved enough to pay off her debts to Sonamukhi as well as the hefty amount that every woman wishing to break free has to pay the brothel owner. She rented a small room in a house three lanes away from Sonamukhi's establishment. It was a teary send-off. Saraju promised to keep visiting Sonamukhi, she owed her so much.

Initially Saraju revelled in being the mistress of her own household. She could decide how to divide her time between work and leisure without an owner's interference. She didn't have to share her income with anyone, could take on babus that she wanted to, and spend all her free time with her child. But it was also a lot harder. At Sonamukhi's house there had been others taking care of the household chores. Saraju could not afford to pay someone else to do that. She expected Malati to help with the rest of the housework. Malati, who had led a pampered life so far, resisted. This soon led to loud disagreements and arguments between them. But much worse, in Saraju's books, was the fact that Malati did not apply herself at school. She was desperate for her daughter to finish school and work far away from the flesh trade. They had ongoing battles about this even when Malati was very young.

Malati was stubborn and soon started finding her own way around Sonagachi. Saraju found out that Malati had started going to Noor Manzil, a brothel that hired young girls to striptease and perform sexually explicit dances. The girls would dance and if the clients wanted more, the 'aunties' who ran the establishment would allot them a room. The girls had to hand over 50 per cent of their earnings to the aunties at the end of each session. The rate charged was much lower for newcomers like college boys who were often low on cash and were happy to sit in a corner and watch. For those who wanted physical contact with the girls, the price was higher. There were different rates for different levels of entertainment.

When Malati was as young as twelve or thirteen, she had struck up a friendship with the aunties and would run small errands for them, pick up essentials from the shops, carry messages, even step in for a sick girl and serve liquor during the day dance sessions.

Noor Manzil gave her a chance to earn her own money…and her independence. But this meant that she often skipped school.

One day when Saraju found out that Malati had not gone to school at all, she was furious.

'Where have you been all day?' Saraju barked when she saw Malati. The girl had just come in, sucking on an ice lolly. She plonked her school bag on the floor and was about to take her nightie from the clothesline that ran across the middle of the room.

'Why?'

'Answer me first. Where were you?'

'School.'

'Don't lie. You didn't go to school today. Where were you and why are you so late?' Saraju demanded.

'School got over early, so I went out with some friends.'

'Went out and did what?'

'Just roamed about aimlessly and came back!'

'No. Your school announced a holiday because an old teacher died. All the others came back home. I spoke to them. You went to Noor Manzil, didn't you?'

'But what would I do after coming back? Your door would have been locked at that time. And I would have had to sit outside and wait!' Malati found her voice.

'You could have come back and chatted with your friend across the veranda. You couldn't have waited for a little while?' Saraju retorted.

'A little while? You were with Manu kaka. You're with him all the time these days. Everyone in the para says that he is your lover. I did not want to disturb you when he is around…' Malati said and reached for the clothesline.

'What did you do at Noor Manzil?' Saraju was adamant.

'N…nothing. Usha told me that they give you money if you run errands for the aunties there.'

'They do that to lure young girls. It's a trap. Do you understand? Stay away from that place if you don't want to land up in a life like me or even worse. Do you want to get sold to some foreigner? You will never be able to see me again…'

'Ma, those mashis are not all that bad. They give us money for helping out.'

'Money, money, money, all the time. What do you need money for? Don't you get food on time? I provide you with everything.'

'Ma, once in a while I like to have puchka and jhaalmuri with my friends, buy colourful clips and ribbons or lozenges and churan. Where will I get money for that?'

'Listen, girl, you don't want to become a prostitute like me. This is the time to study and learn. I want you to study, go as far as you can go from this life, get married to someone on the outside.'

A silence followed. Malati changed into her home clothes and went downstairs to the bathroom to freshen up. By the time she came back, Saraju had brought out the aluminium plates. A big handi full of rice stood in the middle of the room. It was full of panta bhat. There was leftover rice from the previous night on which Saraju had poured water. They ate the rice with onions, chillies, a slice of lemon and some mashed potatoes. Malati sat down to eat; it was well past her usual lunchtime.

But this peace was short-lived. Nothing could stop Malati from going back to Noor Manzil for the quick bucks it promised. For a few years, she kept to the errand-running side of the business. It wasn't as though she didn't dream of a regular married life outside Sonagachi, but she couldn't picture it. She had not seen anything like it in her neighbourhood. And the movies that she saw only made her more confused. She could not imagine a life where just one man had the right over your mind and body, with whom you would have children… In comparison, Noor Manzil looked more real and showed a dream that seemed reachable—enough money to have two square meals a day, and a few treats and pretty clothes once in a while.

Malati was not good-looking in the way that Saraju was, but with her expressive eyes, and her ability to make friends, she was rather popular. She had friends among the boys and girls she grew up with, her schoolmates, and even among those she met during her escapades from school. These outsiders were the ones who expanded her world—they took her to the other posh buildings in Sonagachi. Here, young girls were in demand not just for sex but for other jobs like massages and dance as well. Malati was a good dancer and easily picked up the titillating steps. Those who came to have their fun in these establishments were more affluent than the men who came to her mother's rooms. They enjoyed the excitement of being pampered and titillated by young girls. At first Malati was uncomfortable with the grabbing and touching, but in time she became deft at exciting the clients while avoiding their roving hands.

Malati was happy with this arrangement. Of course, she didn't tell Saraju about any of this. But it wasn't hard for her mother to find out what she was up to. In Sonagachi, nothing remained secret for long. But Noor Manzil was in a different class than the establishments that Saraju was used to. And class distinction was strong here, like in many other places. Some lanes in Sonagachi were considered upper class. Buildings like Noor Manzil and Prem Manzil were more posh-looking multi-storeyed structures that stood apart from the smaller grubby hovels that teemed on most other lanes. They attracted a richer clientele. These upper-class establishments were controlled by veteran aunties and a handful of women who called themselves Agrawalis. They were successors of the original nautch girls of the Raj era. Saraju knew that once Malati had started visiting Noor Manzil, she had very little hope of getting her back on track.

Paltu, the son of one of the women who worked for Sonamukhi, was Malati's closest friend. As kids, when they played house, Malati would invariably be the mother and choose Paltu to be the father. Paltu was neither good-looking nor gregarious, but the fact that he was always there for Malati, never fought with her and quietly accepted her tantrums meant that she grew to depend on him. She knew she could trust Paltu with her deepest, darkest secrets. Some of these were about the crushes she had on the handsome and rich young clients.

'You know what, Paltu, that guy Joy is really good-looking.' Paltu had gone to Noor Manzil to ask Malati to come home—Saraju had sent him. 'He really likes me,' she went on as they walked back home. 'He just sat there all the time, drinking, refusing to even go up to the room with his girl.'

'You be careful, Malati. You don't know how these men can be,' Paltu said.

'What would you know about them? You think such bhadraloks would come to our side of Sonagachi? I'm glad that I started coming to these lanes,' Malati said.

'Just because they look and talk posh doesn't mean they won't try to take advantage of you,' Paltu tried to get Malati to see reason.

'Stop talking like Ma. I can take care of myself,' Malati snapped.

'Please don't get angry, Malati. We both worry about you—.'

'So why don't you get some work that will let you buy whatever I want?' Malati was angry. She sped up, leaving Paltu behind. She had spent the afternoon flirting with Joy, a college boy from a rich family, who often came with his friends. He paid special attention to her, Malati thought. He must be interested in me. What did Paltu know about the good life? All he knows are the slums and rags—a life that she hated.

Paltu tried to catch up with her, pleading with her not to get angry.

'I'm sorry, Malati. Forget I said anything. Let's go share a cold drink,' he said, taking hold of her hand. She shook him off.

'Cool down, Malati. Please,' Paltu said.

Malati finally relaxed a little. 'Okay… No need for drama. I'll have a Thums Up, you can have a smoke. I'll buy you a cigarette. Come on.'

It was not long before Malati became thick with the Joys, Pritams and Kushans—all rich kids who visited Noor Manzil regularly. She was clear that she would not sleep with them, but was open to almost everything else with her chosen few, of course, for a price. She was not alone; there were other young girls like her in these upscale brothels. These girls were not the ones she had grown up with. Girls with backgrounds like hers were discouraged from coming here because they lacked class. Malati realized that she was an exception and this made her feel special.

But one way or the other, things came to a head.

Saraju had gone to get water from the Corporation tap, having asked Malati to complete her homework and cut the vegetables. When Saraju came back nearly two hours later, with a bucket of washed clothes in one hand and water in another, Malati was sitting outside the house and chatting with a neighbour.

'Have you finished your work?' Saraju asked. Malati ignored her mother and continued chatting with her friend.

Saraju went in and saw that Malati's books were still in her schoolbag and the vegetables were lying untouched on the kitchen floor. Saraju snapped. She stormed out and slapped Malati across the face. Malati stared in shock. She hadn't expected her mother to react this way, that too in front of an outsider. She screamed at Saraju.

'How dare you, you slut!'

Saraju got hold of a fistful of Malati's hair and pulled hard. She had never become violent before, but Malati was becoming impossible. Malati pushed her mother away, and ran down the stairs.

'Go! Don't come back to eat off a slut's income,' Saraju yelled after her. She noticed that Malati was crying in rage. But she didn't care. She had been too lenient with an obstinate, ungrateful girl.

Malati didn't return for lunch. Saraju continued her day, taking on three more customers till the evening. Malati had still not returned and Saraju started to get a little worried. She locked her house and went to Sonamukhi's, hoping that Malati might have gone there. She often did after her fights with her mother. But Sonamukhi and the rest of the household had not seen Malati. Saraju looked in the homes of some of her other friends, but no one had heard from her. Saraju started to panic. She went back home and waited anxiously. Malati finally returned in the dead of the night. Saraju was sitting on the stairs weeping. She took one look at Malati and knew that something terrible had happened. Malati hobbled up the stairs to their rooms. She looked to be in great pain. Saraju quietly followed her. Malati crumpled to the floor.

'Who did this to you?' Saraju asked her.

'No one *did* anything, I decided to start my own career,' Malati sneered.

'Why did you do this? How could you?' Saraju asked.

'I wanted to earn.'

'Who was it?'

'There were three of them. Japani fixed them up for me in her room. I didn't know it would hurt so much. I thought they would tear me open,' Malati groaned in pain.

'You fool! You've lost your virginity to a gang rape. I would never have let you get into this sick profession and even if you did, your first night is special, you get paid specially for that…' Saraju yelled at her. 'How much did they pay you?'

Malati opened her fist to show the few small notes she had been clutching tightly all this while.

'That's it? You stupid, stupid girl, ' Saraju stopped herself from saying much more. She was devastated, but she could see that for all her bravado, Malati was shaken.

Soon after, Malati stopped going to school. Saraju could no longer force her to do anything she didn't want to. But it broke her heart that Malati, barely fifteen years old, had gone into the sex business voluntarily. But it did ease their financial burden. Between mother and daughter they ran quite a neat household. Malati loved being able to earn her own money. Unlike most women of Saraju's generation, Malati often went out of Sonagachi with men who were willing to pay more for women who gratified them in locales of their choice rather than in the dingy brothel rooms.

Malati finally felt like she had broken free.

3.

Malati turned fifteen a few months after that incident. A Bengali calendar with a picture of Goddess Lakshmi hung on one of the walls. Saraju would look for Malati's birthday at the beginning of the Bengali New Year on Poila Boishakh and its corresponding English date and put a circle around it with her kajal pencil. She always made payesh for Malati's birthday. Saraju remembered fondly how at Jamtala, every child's birthday was celebrated with payesh. The mothers would make sure to buy extra milk. They would then boil the milk down until it became thick and concentrated. They would add scented rice of the Gobindo Bhog variety to the milk along with cardamom and raisins to make delicious payesh. This, a prayer for a joyous and prosperous year ahead, was a legacy that Saraju had carried with her from her previous life. At Sonagachi, Malati was perhaps the only child whose birthday was celebrated like this. Malati had a sweet tooth and loved payesh.

On Malati's fifteenth birthday, Saraju swept into the tiny room where she slept.

'Still asleep? Wake up, Malati, it's your birthday!' The room was dark and stuffy.

'Uff! Ma, I'm tired.' Malati mumbled and turned to the other side.

'Listen, I have already bathed and made payesh for you. I also bought hot singaras on my way back from the mandir. Get up and splash some water on your face, I'll make tea for us.' Saraju was happy.

Malati mumbled something incoherent, snuggling deeper under the sheet.

'Aiy, Malati, the singaras are getting cold!' Saraju said, throwing open the window. Bright sunlight streamed in. Malati screamed and jumped out of bed.

'How dare you open the window! Don't you realize I'm sleeping?' Malati shouted.

'Sona meye, don't shout and spoil an auspicious day. It's already 9 o'clock and you should be up by now,' Saraju said sternly.

'Why can't you just leave me alone?' Malati said and stormed out of the room and stomped down the stairs to the common bathroom.

Saraju stood there for a moment, closed her eyes tight and sighed. She just couldn't understand Malati and her mood swings. She had turned into a rebel for no reason! Was this what all teenagers were like? She thought back to her own teenage years. Even in the refugee camp, her life had seemed a lot calmer. Saraju went into the tiny kitchen and lit the stove, putting a pot of water on to make tea. She decided not to react to Malati's tantrums for the moment. This worked best with the girl. As the water started to boil, Malati came into the kitchen and sat down on the floor, looking a little glum. But she looked a lot calmer. Saraju was relieved.

She poured the tea, added milk and sugar and, placing the two steaming glasses on the floor, said 'There, have tea, you'll feel better.' Saraju brought out the four singaras on an aluminium plate.

'Why did you do all this?'

'It's a good day! I've also made payesh for you!'

'Why do you take all this trouble every year, Ma? You know I don't care for all this fuss.' Malati said, picking up a singara and sipping the tea. She almost sounded bored.

'You are so young, Malati, why are you so cynical? All this anger will leave a mark on your face in the long run!' Saraju said.

'Ma, I know I neither have your face nor your complexion, but how does that matter? People will come to me not for my face or my colour and you know that,' Malati said getting up abruptly and brushing off the crumbs of the singara from her nightie.

'Why don't you take a bath? Then you can have some payesh, go to the temple, maybe go for a movie with your friends?'

Malati quickly picked up her gamcha and a midi skirt and top that she wore when she went out. Saraju was surprised at her daughter's sudden burst of energy.

'I have many plans for today. Keep the payesh, I will have it later. And don't make anything for dinner. We will have biryani…' Malati said before rushing down the stairs, perhaps heading to the tank where women gathered for their bath through the day. This tank was not dependant on the Corporation's water supply. It was fed directly from the Hooghly by centuries-old pipelines that had been laid during British rule and were surprisingly still functional. Saraju sighed again. She slowly ate the rest of the singaras. She felt sad because she had been hoping that the day would turn out differently, but she should have known, she castigated herself.

Malati was too headstrong and contrary. When had that little girl who demanded cuddles and story time become this prickly young woman? Saraju could not fathom this attitude. The change had come about slowly, and Saraju could no longer resolve it by beating her or using any form of coercion. Even the softest tone of rebuke often caused her to shut down. When Malati sensed the smallest hint of disapproval, she immediately hardened, even becoming self-destructive. Saraju lived in fear of her daughter's volatile temperament.

The wall between mother and daughter had grown firmer. After that disastrous first sexual experience, Saraju hoped that Malati might want to stay home and shun the brothel life. She had secretly thanked God when she found Malati at home for that whole week, unusually quiet and refusing to see even her closest friends. But the effect soon waned and Malati became more adventurous than ever.

◆

It had been a few years since Saraju had struck out on her own, but the bond that she had developed with Sonamukhi had remained strong. Over the years, Sonamukhi had become weaker, and severe arthritis prevented her from moving out of the house. Her frame was huge and lack of movement caused her to gain weight, making it difficult for her to walk even with a walking stick. Though not exactly bed-ridden, she had given over the daily running of the brothel to one of the younger women. Saraju often went to visit her. Like in the old days, she would massage Sonamukhi's feet with warm mustard oil as they talked.

Malati had grown up in this house and had fond memories

of how Sona Dida, and the other women of the household doted on her. While her mother had been busy with clients, they had kept her well fed and suitably entertained. In those early years, she hardly saw her mother, she was brought up by her mashis. Many of these mashis had retired from the trade, some had moved away, some had died from undiagnosed diseases. Some had managed to take up rooms in the vicinity, renting them out to younger women, the less fortunate ones worked as ayahs or maids in rich brothels or the nearby kothis. Malati took care not to visit when her mother was around. She would go alone and sit with Sonamukhi, one of the very few people with whom she felt she could be herself. She would head straight for the tin of narkel naru that Sonamukhi always kept by her bedside. Malati loved the coconut-and-jaggery laddus. When Malati still lived there, she was the only one who was allowed to help herself from the box.

'Arre, Saraju, come in, come in. Where have you been! It's been more than a month now!' Sonamukhi was lying on the mat and fanning herself when Saraju walked in. As Sonamukhi tried to sit up, her face twisted with pain.

'Here, Mashi ma, let me help you,' Saraju said, putting her hand around Sonamukhi and helping her up. Then she adjusted the pillow behind her back.

'How I miss you, Saraju! When you were here, you did your work and looked after me too. Nowadays, the girls have no time for an old woman,' Sonamukhi said with a sigh, happy that her old favourite had come to visit.

'Mashi, it's been a busy time. Our Malati doesn't care for housework, as you know. So I'm trying to do everything. She brings in money from her clients, but does not lift a finger at home. She will never change!' Saraju complained softly.

'This generation is like that, Saraju, self-centred, but at least Malati gives you money. Many girls might not even bother,' Sonamukhi said.

'This life is so short-lived, Mashi. I'm getting older and men are not interested. I'm not making as much as I used to, so I want to earn whatever money I can. I'm growing dependant on Malati,' Saraju said.

'Do you need money, dear?' Sonamukhi asked, gesturing towards her wooden cashbox.

'No, no, Mashi. You have done so much for me. I don't need money now. I have just come to meet you,' Saraju said, covering Sonamukhi's hands with hers.

'It makes me happy that you have not forgotten me. Malati hasn't visited me in a while. Tell her I was looking for her. I think she can help me with something.'

'What is it, Mashi? Can I help?'

'No. Malati is best suited for the job. There is a housewife from the Sunderbans who came to me recently. She must be close to Malati's age. I've sent her to Bula. But she is still sulking and crying and Bula is not able to handle her. I think Malati can help her come around. I'll ask Bula to pay Malati for her time,' Sonamukhi suggested.

'Malati seems to refuse everything that I suggest. I will tell her that you were looking for her. I'm sure she'll come and see you immediately,' Saraju said.

The next morning Malati went over to Sonamukhi's house.

'Sona Dida, Ma said you were looking for me.'

'Malati. Come, come in, dear. Sit here.'

Malati sat down next to Sonamukhi. Once they had got tea

from the nearby tea stall, Sonamukhi asked, 'Malati, do you have a little time on your hands?'

'For you, Dida, of course. What do you need?'

'See, there's a new girl who I bought recently and managed to sell to Bula. But the girl is moping and Bula is just not able to bring her around. You are close in age—maybe you can get through to her?'

'Sure, Dida, I'll go over to Bula mashi's house and see if I can help,' Malati said doubtfully.

The mashis and pimps had many different methods for breaking in new girls. They hardly ever used the soft, understanding approach. So Malati wasn't sure how she could help.

She went over, expecting to see to see an adamant girl fighting and arguing, looking to escape. But what she found was a soft, plump woman, rather lovely to look at. Her eyes and nose were red and her face was drawn, clearly she had been crying. She was meekly going about the household chores, helping the other women clean their rooms and get dressed.

'Malati!' Bula was happy to see her. 'Sona Didi must have sent you, right?'

'Yes, Mashi. Can I help?'

'Malati, this is Golapi. She's not able to make her peace with her new life. Explain to her that this is where she has to make her life. I'll pay you for your time, dear. I know you've become a busy woman,' Bula said.

'But, Mashi, that could take a lot of time. This girl was not born here, she looks like she's from a middle-class family.' Golapi was wearing a big red bindi, vermilion had stained the parting in her hair, and she was wearing the shankha-pola on her wrists—all signs of a married woman. Malati was sceptical about being able to get through to Golapi.

'Just try please, Malati. I don't think rough treatment will be the right way to go. And you've been mixing with people from outside. I think you will be able to talk to her,' Bula insisted.

◆

Golapi was shocked at the sudden change in her life that had brought her to Sonagachi, but it wasn't as though her earlier life had been a happy one. Golapi's parents, though not poor, did not have the money that her in-laws demanded. They had not paid the dowry they had promised even a year after the wedding. Golapi had been a fun-loving young woman. She had tried to win her husband and his family over. She took on the entire housework soon after marriage. But her mother-in-law and husband took turns berating and beating her for the smallest mistakes. Just another dowry story.

A whiff of hope came in with Golapi's widowed sister-in-law, Asha. Asha began visiting their house and quickly befriended the isolated Golapi. Asha would often take on Golapi's mother-in-law when she started criticizing her daughter-in-law. Gradually a bond developed between them and Golapi confided in Asha. A few months after befriending Golapi, Asha offered to take her to see a fair near Domjur in Howrah. Golapi was so excited at this unexpected treat that she didn't notice how readily her mother-in-law gave permission. She even encouraged her son to give Golapi some money to spend at the fair. The day before they were to leave, Golapi opened her trunk that held her few saris and started to pack.

'Didi, please take a look and tell me which one I should wear at the fair,' she asked Asha.

'Wear the pink one, it goes with your name. Golapi…pinky!' Asha joked and Golapi blushed.

'Don't take too many clothes. That heavy bag will slow you down,' Asha told Golapi with a grin.

'Didi, how many days are we staying? Where will we spend the night?'

'You don't worry about anything. Leave all that to me. And don't worry about your in-laws. I have managed everything. I've spoken to your husband and he has explained to his mother. Get ready to have fun for once.'

Golapi couldn't contain her wide smile.

The next day, Asha and Golapi set off early in the morning, first on the bus to the local train station and from there they took the Diamond Harbour train to Sealdah. After the initial excitement, Golapi became lulled by the motion of the train. The scenery rushing past outside, the cool breeze against her face, everything seemed so unreal. No one chided her to hurry up with the scrubbing of the utensils or washing of the clothes, no chopping of vegetables, no cooking to be done… No one was cuffing her or threatening violence. Bliss…she thought, savouring every moment. But when the Diamond Harbour local pulled up at Sealdah, she was shaken. The crowd at the Sealdah station sounded like a roaring ocean to her. Golapi had never seen so many people—pushing, jostling and running in all directions.

'Didi, what a crowd! I'll get lost in that.'

'Don't worry. Let's just wait until the crowd thins out.'

'What if the train leaves?'

Asha laughed at her naive sister-in-law.

'This is the last station. The train will stay here for some time before starting on its return journey. You sit still and do exactly as I tell you. I'll go buy us some tea. Here, have this singara and I'll come back with the tea,' Asha produced the newspaper-wrapped snack from her bag and handed it to Golapi. She then got off the train and walked towards the food stalls on the platform. Golapi was hungry and ate the singara as she waited for Asha. Slowly, the crowd in the compartment thinned out, and she was the only one left. Golapi peered out of the window, trying to catch a glimpse of Asha. But she couldn't see her. Golapi started to feel uneasy. Her limbs felt loose and there was a queasy feeling in her stomach. She felt dizzy. She tried to reach for the water bottle but found she couldn't move her arms. That was the last memory she had of the train.

When Golapi gained consciousness, she found herself lying on the floor of a room. All around her were half-dressed girls who were chatting as they put on make-up. She was groggy and her head was heavy. She looked around hoping to see Asha, but couldn't lift her head off the bed sheet. She fell unconscious once more.

Many hours later, Golapi came to her senses. When she opened her eyes, she saw nothing that was familiar. Golapi had never before been alone anywhere, without her parents or her husband's family. She was frozen in fear. She didn't try to run away or protest or demand an explanation. She just sat on the sheet and shivered until her bladder seemed about to burst. She stared at the girls around her. Some had their petticoats tied above their breasts. They were putting on make-up and chatting. They cracked crass jokes and used foul language, something that Golapi had never heard women do. Finally she spoke up.

'Didi, I want to visit the toilet...' she said feebly to the girl nearest to her. The girl was finishing with her eye liner and looked down at Golapi through the mirror that was on the shelf in front of her.

'Oh! Good you woke up. We thought we'd have to call a doctor!' The girl turned to Golapi. Golapi could see now that she was about the same age as her, but the make-up made her look older.

'Didi, where's the toilet? I badly need to go.'

'Downstairs. Go down the staircase at the end of the passage and ask someone.'

Golapi tried to get up but her legs felt like rubber and she stumbled, tripping over the end of her sari. The girl saw that Golapi was unsteady and rushed forward to help.

'Wait, wait. Don't fall and hurt yourself. I'll come with you,' the girl said. Then she helped Golapi down the stairs.

'Didi, where am I? Where is Asha didi?'

'Asha? There is no one in Sonamukhi mashi's house by that name. You are in Sonagachi, don't you know?'

'Sonagachi? Where is that? I was going to Domjur to attend a fair with Asha didi. She's my sister-in-law.'

'Same old story. The toilet is in there. There's water in a drum. Wash your face. I'll wait, but don't be long. My customer will be here any moment,' the girl showed her the dark, rank toilet with a sack doing duty as the door.

Golapi was grateful to use the toilet, but almost immediately panic gripped her. Where had she ended up? What would her husband and mother-in-law do to her if they found out where she had spent the night? How was she going to get back home? She came out to find the girl waiting for her.

'Didi, I think I'm lost. Please help me get back home. My

husband will be so angry with me…' Golapi started crying.

'Tchk…tchk…Crying won't help. It's not such a bad life here, after all.' The girl led Golapi to a room on the ground floor where Sonamukhi sat talking to a man. On seeing the two girls at the door, she dismissed the man.

'Come in, Golapi. Protima, you go do your work.' Golapi listened as Protima's footsteps faded away.

Sonamukhi was eager to welcome the new inmate to her brothel. She waved the girl to come closer and sit on the mattress next to her. 'This is your temporary home till I find a better one for you, Golapi. I hope you will learn to be happy in Sonagachi,' Sonamukhi said. Golapi started weeping.

'Mashi ma, I can't make out what is going on. I left home with my sister-in-law to go to a fair at Domjur. We were on the train and then…and then…I don't know how I came here. Please help me. I have to go home,' Golapi sobbed.

Sonamukhi drew on her reserves of patience. After all, Golapi was not the first girl that she had bought from the outside or the first who had been sold by her family.

'Golapi, you are in Sonagachi and not in Domjur. This is a red-light area where girls live by selling sex. All you have to do is entertain your customers. We will teach you how. You know the basics as a married woman, but there's so much more…' Sonamukhi explained.

Golapi buried her face in her hands and started sobbing louder. Sonamukhi sighed.

'Mashi ma, I have never harmed anyone, why did such ill fate strike me?' Golapi held on to Sonamukhi's feet in desperation.

'Who told you that you are ill-fated? It's how you look at life. Were you happy at home? Was there even one day when you weren't shouted at? Your family got rid of you for money. That woman you call Asha didi is an agent and your in-laws knew that. They wanted to get rid of you so that your husband can marry a girl who will bring a hefty dowry.

Golapi was so shocked that she stopped sobbing and stared at Sonamukhi in horror. The people who were supposed to protect her had not only thrown her out, they had sold her like cattle.

Sonamukhi pressed her advantage, seeing that she had got through to the young woman. 'They could have killed you and claimed a cylinder explosion or some other accident. Do you know how many women die that way? You are alive, you will be fed and clothed, you will get to make friends. Many women would consider that fortunate. Forget your family and adjust to this new life. And, believe me, you will do well. With your smooth complexion, voluptuous figure and pretty face… I have to send you to your new home soon but remember my words and you will be happy,' Sonamukhi said, softening a bit and using the pallu of her sari to wipe Golapi's tears.

'I'm scared…' was all Golapi managed to say.

'Don't be. If you are able to shake off your inhibitions, you will enjoy yourself and earn well. Trust me,' Sonamukhi said, at her motherly best.

Golapi cried silently and stared at the floor in disbelief.

'Hey! What are you girls staring at?' Sonamukhi turned towards the door to shoo away some of the girls who were crowding the entrance, curious about the latest outsider.

In a few days, Sonamukhi sold Golapi on to Bula. Golapi's first few days at Bula's household were no different. She did not protest and even willingly helped out with the housework following instructions. But Bula needed Golapi to start working.

She had paid a lot to Sonamukhi and needed to start earning on her investment. Shouting at Golapi had proved to be useless. The girl was too used to being shouted at and was more terrified of the sex work than physical beatings. Bula realized that the harsh method would be the wrong approach to take with this girl. She asked Sonamukhi to suggest a remedy and that is how Malati got involved.

Rude and selfish Malati seemed to take to Golapi at once. The younger woman called Malati 'didi' and was almost deferential. Slowly, they formed a close bond.

Within a few weeks, all signs of shock and depression vanished and Golapi made her peace with her new lot in life. She didn't have any tedious household chores, she wasn't beaten, got to eat good food, was waited on. She could never bring herself to think too much about the time she spent with her customers. And from a timid, shaken village girl, Golapi turned into a head-turner at Sonagachi.

Golapi had been with Bula for just three months when her life changed once again. With everything that was new and confusing in her life, Golapi hadn't been paying attention to herself. It was only when Golapi missed her fourth period that she realized in horror that she was pregnant. She hadn't been showing the usual signs of early pregnancy. In the short time that she had been here, Golapi had turned herself into Bula's favourite with Malati's help. Golapi would massage Bula's feet, chat with her, run to get her an extra cushion or her paandaan. Golapi had also started earning well and Bula knew that she would get better and be able to get more and richer clients. But Golapi had also learned that Sonagachi operated under strict rules. Physical ailments were not looked upon kindly. And pregnancy was not allowed unless there was a babu to sponsor it. Though Golapi had already become popular among the regulars at Bula's brothel, she was too new to have a regular babu. Moreover, it was a pregnancy that she had probably carried with her from home and Bula would not allow her to keep the baby. Golapi knew she was in deep trouble. She needed to talk to Malati.

Golapi caught up with Malati who was walking down to the Corporation tap to fill water. There was a long queue and they stood chatting. It was a hot and humid day and Golapi was sweating profusely. She started to feel light-headed. She walked over to sit in the shade.

'What happened? The heat is getting to you?' Malati asked, looking at Golapi in surprise.

'No...' said Golapi weakly. Malati was horrified to see that her friend had slowly leaned over and collapsed to the ground.

'Golapi!' Malati lunged and caught her before her head hit the ground. The other women gathered around them.

'Protima, get some water. This girl has blacked out...' Malati said, fanning Golapi's face with her pallu.

Protima filled some water in a bottle and handed it to Malati. Malati sprinkled some water on Golapi's face, and continued fanning her.

'She didn't seem unwell even a few minutes ago,' Protima said.

'Hope we don't have to call the doctor,' Malati said.

'That would mean a lot of money! Will her mashi allow that? Even compounder Gopal takes twenty rupees to look at girls and give medicines,' Protima looked concerned.

'I'll talk to Bula mashi if that's necessary,' Malati said.

Golapi came to slowly, but couldn't get up. With great effort she lifted her head and vomited. The women around her gasped, they knew what these symptoms meant. It was never good news for the young girls in Sonagachi.

'How many periods have you missed, Golapi?' Malati asked sympathetically, putting an arm around the sick girl as she fought to catch her breath.

'Three... I think. Maybe four...'

'You stupid girl,' hissed Protima. 'Why didn't you tell your mashi when you missed it the first time? That's the rule here. The bigger the baby grows inside you, the greater the risk.'

'Let's not scare her anymore. She's not familiar with our rules here,' said Malati, as she calculated mentally, coming to the conclusion that the baby was probably Golapi's husband's.

'What will happen to me?' Golapi finally managed to say feebly. She was ashen.

'We'll take care of it,' Malati tried to sound reassuring. 'If you've missed three or four periods, that means that the baby is quite big, so pills won't work. You will have to go to a clinic for a wash up!' Malati said.

'Can't I keep the baby?' Golapi asked hesitantly.

'Don't you dare say that to Mashi or she will kill you,' Malati said briskly. 'I'm coming with you. Mashi likes me too. Let me talk to her. We'll figure this out,' Malati said with all the confidence she could muster.

Golapi simply hugged her and started weeping.

'Didi, they used to beat me up and my husband hated me for not bringing him the promised dowry. If they hadn't sold me off, they would have probably burnt me one day or I would have hanged myself. I have nothing but hate for them. But still, this baby will be my real home. Malati, you are my only friend here...

please help me keep the child…please,' Golapi pleaded.

Malati was silent for a while. She was reminded of the story that she had heard many years ago…of how her mother had fought tooth and nail to keep her…though under slightly different circumstances. Despite the chasm that was growing between her and her mother, she felt for her and for her friend. In so many ways, Golapi would never become as hardened as the other girls who had grown up in Sonagachi. She was like Saraju in that sense.

'It's a lot more difficult than you think, but I will still try,' Malati promised. She enlisted the support of her mother and Sona Dida and managed to convince Bula to let Golapi keep the baby. In any case, the pregnancy was so far along that any attempt to get rid of it would have been too dangerous. Bula knew that the loss incurred by letting Golapi carry the pregnancy to term could be overcome. Golapi was young and had plenty of earning potential. Golapi promised to work twice as hard to make up for all the time lost. Malati helped by paying some of her income towards this.

Five months later, a healthy baby boy was born to Golapi. Malati named him Prateek.

4.

Malati groaned and opened her eyes. She felt sick, she was seriously ill. Her arms and legs felt heavy, and she could barely open her eyes. Saraju bustled about, getting ready for the day.

'Wake up, Malati. It's nearly 10 o'clock!'

Malati grunted and pulled herself out of bed. She made her way unsteadily to the kitchen. Saraju placed two glasses of tea on the floor.

'Ma, I don't want tea.'

'You've barely been eating for days now. Do you have a fever?' Saraju asked, feeling her daughter's forehead.

'No, I feel strange. Weak, out of breath. I don't feel like eating anything. The smell of food is making me sick.'

Saraju's breath caught in her throat. 'When did you last have your period?' she asked sharply.

Malati tried to calculate. She had lost track. Malati had become reckless. She negotiated her rate fiercely, and slept with as many men as she felt like. Some of them were Joy's friends, rich boys who thought they were slick, but were raucous, awkward. Others were middle-aged men who came to Sonagachi looking for young girls. In her desperate attempt to take back control of her life, she had lost track of the men and of herself. She had suspected for some days that she was in trouble. Getting confirmation from her mother made the bile rise up in her throat.

She groaned softly and leaned against the wall.

'Malati, please visit Leela di with me. She will see if medicines can help you. Maybe it's not too late to do something,' Saraju beseeched her.

Malati didn't want a baby! She was too young for this responsibility.

She agreed, silently hoping that Leela, one of the midwives of Sonagachi, would find a solution for her as she had for so many other women.

◆

Malati screamed as Leela thrust almost her entire arm into her. Malati was lying on a hard, grimy table, naked from the waist down, her legs held apart. Leela had rinsed her hand in hot water, and plunged one hand into her while she felt her stomach with the other. So far, Malati had followed instructions, believing that some pain and discomfort was the price to pay to rid herself of the problem. But she could stand it no longer.

'Chup, chup...let her do her job,' Saraju shushed her daughter.

'Oi Ma...she's killing me!'

'Shut up now. She has to pull it out, she can't do that with you squirming.'

'Pull it out!' Mad with panic, Malati kicked out and extricated herself. She lurched to her feet.

'Malati, behave yourself! Didi, please don't mind her,' Saraju pleaded, trying to force Malati back onto the table.

Malati broke down in terror. 'Ma, I don't want this butchery. I'll take the medicine.'

Saraju relented. Leela had helped many women, but Saraju also knew of too many women who had bled to death after her interventions.

So they took the medicines from Leela and went home. Malati diligently took the medication and hoped and prayed. But the child had taken root inside her, and the medicines had no effect. Despite repeated attempts, the baby remained ensconced in her womb, growing. Malati had no choice but to come to terms with it but she could not make herself love or even want the child.

This parasite, she thought to herself. She was determined not to let it change her life. It didn't matter that Malati hated the creature growing inside her—it grew bigger and made her easily tired. She was sitting at the door one evening, dreaming and dozing when Paltu walked up.

It had been weeks since she had seen him, she realized.

Paltu sat next to her. 'Look at your state,' he said quietly.

'Is that why you haven't come to see me? It's been so long,' Malati retorted sharply.

Paltu didn't answer at once. Neither Saraju nor Malati had told him about the pregnancy or the earlier rape that had started Malati down this path, but he knew something was up. He had tried very hard to convince Malati that the young men she thought were so cool were men after all. That strutting peacock Joy had turned out to be much worse than Paltu feared. He was sure that the baby was his. Ever since they had been children, Paltu had looked out for Malati. She was brash and careless and he felt like he had to be her armour. He even stood up to Saraju when she and Malati argued. But once Malati started up with those rich boys, he had been out of his depth. He blamed himself, but he also blamed Malati and her hankering for the good life.

'How did a clever girl like you fall into a trap?' he finally asked.

'Oh! Shut up. It was an accident. But this monster is not going to change my life,' Malati said acridly.

'It's that rich brat from the kothi, right?'

Malati didn't confirm his suspicions. 'Paltu, don't be jealous. I know whose sin I'm carrying, but I will not tell you.'

'I'm not jealous Malati, I just feel miserable looking at you. Let me at least talk to the guy so that he gives you some money to get you through the next few months. He's rich enough, isn't he? Lives in one of those big posh buildings…'

'Paltu, you're making assumptions because of your jealousy. Listen, don't squeeze a lemon too hard, it will become bitter. Let's make the best of things and do what we can for each other,' Malati said deliberately.

'I'll do what I can for you, Malati. I'll take care of you…and the child,' Paltu said.

'How are you going to do that?' Malati retorted.

'I'll do any work, I'll provide for you—'

Malati was uncharacteristically gentle. 'Paltu, you're not going to earn enough by running errands for the aunties. I will provide for myself. You don't want to yoke yourself to me and this child of sin. Walk with me,' she said heaving herself up with some effort. 'Japani has lined up some clients for me—men with specific tastes.'

'You're going to sleep with men in your condition?' he asked, aghast.

Months ago, Saraju had encouraged Paltu to talk to Malati, find out who the father of the child was, and how Malati was planning on getting him to provide some money. But Paltu had been struggling with his jealousy. Saraju would have been happy to see Malati settle down with him. He was an honest boy, though somewhat weak compared to her headstrong daughter. Saraju's dream of breaking Malati out of the trade and away from Sonagachi had been crushed.

Malati's assessment of Paltu was not quite the same as her mother's. She thought of him as a friend but could not see him as her provider or husband. Malati was self-sufficient and was capable of providing for herself without the aid of a male partner, who would become possessive and want to take control of her sex life. She enjoyed the company of the rich young men she met and had sex with. Paltu had no education, no special skills, no real knowledge of the world outside the red-light district, no way to make enough money to feed three mouths, never mind the luxuries that she dreamed of.

But she appreciated that he was devoted to her. He helped Malati put on her sandals and walked with her in silence. All his carefully thought-out arguments to discourage Malati from being with other men blew away in the cool evening breeze.

◆

Saraju walked into the house, fanning herself. The days were hot and sultry and she had spent the morning chatting with Sonamukhi. She used the loose end of her sari to wipe her face and neck. Malati walked down the stairs carrying the dry clothes from the terrace. It was the eighth month of her pregnancy and she was heavy and round. The hot weather was wearing on her. She had not managed to set up any permanent lovers who might have helped pay for the time she would have to take for her pregnancy. Saraju had tried to increase her income, but she was in her thirties, her worth was on the wane. Men wanted their whores young and pretty.

'Shouldn't you be a little more careful now?' Saraju asked her.

'Who is going to wash and dry my clothes then?' Malati snapped, breathless.

'Malati, I have told you I'll take care of it all. Why don't you listen?'

'Even when I brought in my share of the money, you tried to control me. I don't like to be a burden. I hate this confinement!'

'But you can't wish it away, can you? Most women in our lanes don't have their mothers to depend on, you should consider yourself lucky!'

'Lucky? What about this situation is lucky? My life is fucked!'

'Don't use such language,' admonished Saraju. Despite all her years in Sonagachi, she couldn't put up with foul language from her daughter.

'Fucked, fucked, fucked… Don't behave like a Sati Savitri. We were born to be fucked and I have been quite royally fucked, haven't I?' Malati fumed, flinging her clothes onto the cot.

'Don't be silly. The baby has not sinned,' Saraju argued, knowing fully well that she was sowing the seeds of a heated fight. She bit her tongue to stop herself from saying anything more. The girl had ignored every bit of advice that she had given her. Now she was not willing to pay the price.

'Don't talk rubbish. It is a monster, sucking out my life and killing my livelihood,' Malati spat.

'Births and deaths are not in our hands, Malati. Was Kamsa, the demon king, able to kill baby Krishna? Devaki knew that her brother would kill her child. But she still gave birth to her children. She had faith in God, so should you,' Saraju said philosophically.

'I should not have stopped Leela mashi. It would have hurt horribly but I would have been free thereafter. I am paying dearly for my weakness that day,' Malati said slowly.

'It's your karma, Malati. It is better that you accept the living being inside you and feel happy. It's a matter of a month now. Try and rest. Once the baby is born, I'll take care of it. You can go back to living your life,' Saraju tried her best to calm down her daughter.

'I will go on taking customers till the last day, I hope my womb ruptures and the foetus slips out before it is born,' Malati said. Her anger and bitterness were a shock to Saraju.

Malati had expanded her business outside the confines of Sonagachi. It started with her rich clients from Noor Manzil who would take her to hotels, resorts, movie theatres, and on taxi rides. Now that she was pregnant, she was going with the not-so-rich to much cheaper places as well. She attended to customers in cheap cinema halls and at the many ghats of the Hooghly in the dead of the night. Even when her pregnancy started showing, she did not stop. She decided to make use of it by taking on lustful goats who paid to have sex with pregnant women. Because pregnant women could not keep the weight of the men on them for too long, they compensated by allowing myriad other innovative positions.

Malati was being reckless, nearly trying to kill her baby. So it was a miracle that her baby survived after all.

◆

Malati was at home resting. According to Leela the baby would come any day now. That had not stopped Malati from taking on customers. She had already been with three men and had made a decent earning that day. So when a pimp sent her word that one of her special customers was asking for her, she could have refused. Her feet were bloated, her back ached and the baby had been moving and kicking, almost agitated. But this client who had a thing for pregnant women paid double the usual amount. She was thinking of the weeks after the baby was born when she would not be able to make any money. She heaved herself up, knuckled her back and set off. Saraju quickly sent word to Paltu to go after Malati. She was worried that Malati would give birth on the way and wouldn't have anyone to help her. The pimp was a heartless fool, he would run at the first hint of trouble.

Malati made her way to a room attached to a ration shop near Kumartuli, not too far from her home. The young boy that Saraju had sent running had not been able to find Paltu immediately. When he finally made his way to the ration shop, the pimp sneered at him and said that Malati was already with her customer. Paltu ignored him and lit a cigarette, standing in the doorway of the tailoring shop opposite the ration shop. He had stood there many times in the past month, waiting. He had walked Malati to her next appointment or (with relief) back home. He had stopped trying to reason with her after she had blown up at him one too many times. But this time it was different.

Paltu heard a piercing scream from inside the shop.

'Ahh, get off me!' Malati screamed.

Malati had been having sex with this man regularly. He had

latched on to her after her pregnancy became apparent in the sixth month. As he was thrusting and grunting, she felt a sharp pain in her lower abdomen and something trickling out of her vagina. For a few seconds she didn't understand what the sensation was. Then she realized that her waters had broken! She tried her best to stop the man, but he was wild with lust.

'Scream louder…harder…louder…yes…scream till I come…' he showed no signs of letting up.

Malati's breath caught with the pain and she felt a sharp and long contraction. She screamed, hoping to shock the man into stopping. Paltu froze for a few seconds, not sure if that was a scream of pain or pleasure. He didn't want to burst in and be berated for interrupting Malati with a client. But as her screams grew louder he realized that she was in trouble. He banged on the door.

'Malati! What's the matter?'

'Paltu! Get me out of here,' Malati screamed from inside.

'Open up you bastard or I will break the door,' Paltu started banging on the door.

Finally, the man opened the door. Paltu pushed him to the floor and stormed into the room.

Malati was lying on the bed, breathless, her clothes damp—her waters had broken. She was groaning in pain. Paltu knew that Malati had to be taken to a hospital immediately. The baby was coming now. He turned around to face the man squarely. Though frail and short compared to his adversary, Paltu had lost his fear and uncertainty.

'You bastard, are you trying to kill her?' Paltu screamed at the man.

'I didn't realize she was crying in pain!'

'We have to get her to a hospital immediately!'

'So do it...take her!'

'You will come help me take her to the hospital now, no one else is going to,' Paltu was desperate. Malati had stopped screaming and was whimpering in pain.

'Me? I'm not taking her anywhere,' the man retorted, trying to scramble out the door.

'Yes, you are. You are responsible for this mess. Now if you don't get up and help, I will leave her here and go away. If she dies, you will be in deeper shit. Do you understand? I will go straight to the thana and file a complaint against you...the OC knows me...' Paltu said aggressively.

The mention of the police did the trick and the man was deflated, his bluster gone. He went with Paltu to convince a cycle van driver to take Malati to the hospital. The two of them carried Malati to the back of the van. Paltu placed her on the van and made the man sit next to her. He implored the van puller to pedal faster. Paltu ran along as the cycle van wound its way to the hospital.

Malati had lost consciousness by the time they pulled up at the emergency ward of the SRC Hospital at Sealdah. Even in the dead of the night the hospital was crowded with patients and their families. Many sat on the ground outside, waiting their turn.

When they finally got a stretcher and took Malati in, the doctors took one look and proclaimed her dead. Paltu insisted that he had felt her move and implored the doctors to take another look. One young doctor took pity on him and examined Malati again. He found a weak pulse and ordered them to wheel her into the operation theatre.

Paltu, feeling helpless and extremely worried, was sitting outside the OT. He was relieved when Saraju walked in. Paltu had sent word to her and Saraju had rushed to the hospital. The two of them waited, worried sick about Malati's state.

When the tiny underweight little girl was born three hours later, no one believed that she would make it. Weak babies did not have a very good chance of surviving in a poorly equipped government hospital. The baby weighed under one kilo when she was born and, for the first three days, Malati was not able to nurse her. She was weak and barely conscious. The nurses took the baby to other new mothers for feeding but she was too weak to suck. The doctors told Malati to pump breast milk and feed the baby drop by drop at short intervals. Saraju offered to sit with the baby day and night to make sure she was fed.

Malati had lost a lot of blood and needed a transfusion. While Saraju sat with the baby at Malati's bedside and tried to encourage her to feed the baby, Paltu ran around arranging for blood from the blood bank. But Malati was semi-conscious and couldn't comprehend all that her mother was saying to her. On the fifth day, when Malati finally gained consciousness and was told that she had given birth to a baby girl who was fighting for her life, she just turned away.

'Malati, the baby is rather weak, we're trying to get her to feed,' Saraju said softly in Malati's ears.

'Ma, when will they release me?' Malati asked.

'You need more blood, Malati, the doctor says you're very weak.'

'I just want to go home, I'll get better there,' she insisted. 'I want to speak to the doctor when he comes tomorrow.'

'I'll talk to him, don't worry. Malati, at least try to take the baby to your breast. She needs to feel her mother's skin.'

'Why are you wasting time on her? She's not going to live.'

Malati closed her eyes and drifted off.

Saraju was sad that even after having seen the baby, Malati's attitude hadn't undergone a change. But she stayed persistent and tried to get Malati to hold the baby and try to feed her. Her heart went out to the little helpless being who was holding on even when the doctors and her own mother seemed to have given up. She prayed to God everyday, clutching the cloth-wrapped bundle, trying to keep the baby warm.

Finally the baby let out a weak wail one morning and Saraju could not believe her ears. She had been standing at the window with the baby. Holding the baby close to her chest, she rushed to Malati's bedside.

'Malati! Malati, look, your baby is alive! She is crying!'

Malati turned her face away, but Saraju shook Malati in her excitement.

'Malati, you are a mother now and this little creature is your daughter! She's God's gift to you...take her, try to give her some milk. Hold her close to you. She needs you now. God willing, she will live!' Saraju was so happy that tears streamed down her face.

Very gingerly and with shaking hands, Malati accepted the tiny creature and tried to hold her to her breast with Saraju's help. The baby made a faint effort at sucking. Malati's expression softened as she watched her daughter stick out her pink tongue. But the baby was still weak and couldn't latch on—Malati lost patience after a few tries and handed the baby back to her mother and went back to sleep. Saraju did not give up. Every time Malati could sit up, she tried to encourage her to feed the baby.

Because of this long stay in the hospital, the bills had piled up and Saraju was getting panicky. How would they pay so much? Paltu browbeat the man who had been with Malati when she went into labour till he agreed to pay for the hospital. When Malati was finally discharged from the hospital on the tenth day, he was forced to pay the bills and hand over money for the medicines Malati needed after she went home.

5.

Saraju and Paltu brought Malati and the baby home. Malati was still very weak and spent most of the day in bed, sleeping. She felt strange every time she looked at the little creature. It looked ill-formed and almost ugly to her. After having tried a few times, she refused to nurse it and told Saraju not to bother her. The initial pangs of guilt were soon replaced by loathing and irritation. She had handed over her daughter to the permanent care of her mother.

The baby was tiny and weak and the doctors had told Saraju that she would not survive. Saraju had fallen in love with the tiny baby and was determined to keep her alive. She wrapped the baby in old, soft cotton saris, placed her in a small shoebox and put a lamp next to the makeshift crib to keep her warm. The baby was still not able to feed, so Saraju dipped a piece of cloth in cow's milk and fed her, drop by drop. Slowly, the baby started to gain weight and strength and was able to take her feed from a bottle. She is a survivor, Saraju said to herself and looked up to the heavens above with hands folded in gratitude.

When the doctors had given up on the child, Saraju promised a special offering to the Goddess Lakshmi if she kept her granddaughter safe. Now that she was thriving, Saraju named the child after the benevolent goddess.

'She is indeed Lakshmi, look at her tiny, pink and beautifully shaped feet!' Saraju said proudly.

'Ma, she is Lakshmi indeed. As a girl, she will be the one to feed us one day, won't she?' Malati said, cruelly.

'I forbid it, Malati! She is an innocent angel and I will protect her from this evil world.'

'Best of luck, Ma, but I don't see any other future for her. No girl born in Sonagachi can escape its darkness,' Malati said as she lined her eyes with kohl. She had recovered her strength alongside her daughter and was ready to start living her life again.

'You need to have a will to do that. I couldn't change your destiny, but the world will have to go through me to touch Lakshmi,' Saraju snapped. Why was this girl always so cynical! How could any mother behave the way Malati behaved, Saraju thought.

'Ma, no one can change anyone's destiny. I too was born an innocent girl, much like your Lakshmi, right? So what went wrong? Sex fills the air of this place and you inhale it with every breath. You are infected at birth,' Malati said. She put on a bright lipstick, glanced in the mirror and left.

Saraju sighed quietly. Lakshmi gurgled and Saraju smiled, turning to coo to her, and the rest of the world melted away.

◆

'What if I had died that night, Dimma?' Lakshmi said as she entwined herself around Saraju's legs. At five, she was full of questions, mischief and a curiosity about everything around her.

'Death take your enemy!' Saraju admonished her.

Lakshmi was fascinated by the story of her birth. 'Tell me about how you kept me in a box.'

'Yes, like a little kitten. In my village in Jamtala, I would raise kittens in shoeboxes. I raised you just like that,' Saraju would laugh.

'And my mother wasn't able to feed me, so you would soak a cotton cloth in milk and squeeze the drops in my mouth…'

'Yes! And look at you now. How that scraggy baby has grown into such a big, lovely girl!'

The two would spend hours chatting with each other. Saraju's work and her income from it was dwindling. She was past her prime and the household was largely dependent on Malati's earnings. So, barring some loyal clients whom she still entertained, Saraju spent her time looking after the child.

Lakshmi loved it when people called her beautiful. Her grandmother would often say that she was an embodiment of Goddess Lakshmi. Every Thursday, the day of Goddess Lakshmi, Saraju would paint Lakshmi's feet with alta. That day was special to both of them. Saraju would make special offerings to the goddess, with batasha or nokul dana, and then read the *Lakshmir Broto Katha*. Lakshmi loved the weekly ritual and waited patiently for her share of the prasad after the prayers. Her favourite, however, was the narkel naru Saraju made with coconut shavings bound with jaggery.

Being able to care for Lakshmi felt like a second chance to Saraju. When Malati had been a child, she had not been able to spend much time with her. For one thing, they had lived at Sonamukhi's house and Saraju was busy most of the time. Malati was brought up by a bevy of aunties. This time around, Saraju got to spend all her time with Lakshmi. She would bathe her, oil her hair, wash her clothes, feed her, play with her, teach her…

Saraju would often tell the little girl that she should go to school, study hard and take up a job in an office. She had vowed to give her granddaughter a decent life, something that she had once dreamt for Malati. When Lakshmi was three years old, Saraju enrolled her in a crèche run by an NGO for the children of the locality. Saraju would drop her there at 10 a.m. and pick her up after three hours. During this time, she would try and finish all the housework and perhaps entertain a customer.

Malati would wake up by midday and start fixing her appointments for the evening. Once in a while she did visit the upscale apartments like before, but she successfully brought many clients out of these places to rooms rented on hourly basis in the lanes of Sonagachi. There was no denying that these rooms were not as comfortable as the ones Noor Manzil had, but they were not as bad as the ones in which a majority of Sonagachi lived and practised sex work. Malati chose carefully, keeping in mind the background of her clients.

But despite her boundless energy and popularity with the clients, there were days when Malati did have to stay home, something she despised. She hated to do the housework that Saraju expected her to help with and dreaded spending time with the demanding Lakshmi. No amount of scolding and snapping could keep Lakshmi out of Malati's hair.

Once, Saraju insisted that Malati be the one to bring Lakshmi back from the crèche.

'Oof, Ma! Can't I rest for a day?' she complained.

'Malati, the child will love it. She hardly gets to see you!'

'So what? Have I left her wanting for anything? She is cared for, fed well, goes to school, what else does she want?'

'That's all very well, but she is a child and craves her mother's love. It's sad that you don't realize that yourself.'

Malati didn't answer. She uncoiled her bun and combed out her hair.

'Lakshmi sees all the other mothers going to fetch their children. Go now, the crèche will get over in the next fifteen minutes…' Saraju rushed her daughter out the door.

Lakshmi was thrilled to see Malati at the crèche gates and ran to her. She held onto Malati's finger and danced her way back from school. Even Malati was swept up in the child's joy. As they passed the ice-cream vendor, she asked Lakshmi if she wanted an ice cream. Saraju was indulgent but very strict about treats. Lakshmi was thrilled.

'Yes, Ma. Can I have an orange ice lolly?' she chirped happily.

'Okay, go get one. I'll pay,' Malati stopped by the ice-cream cart.

Lakshmi chose her lolly and once she got it, started eating it happily. Some of the other children from the crèche joined with their mothers. Malati stood at a distance and let her be until she finished her ice cream. The sun was beating down hard and it was hot, but for once Malati was patient.

But there was only so much she could take. Once they were home, Lakshmi demanded that Malati change her clothes and feed her. That done, she refused to go to sleep and insisted that Malati play Ludo with her.

'Ma, one game, please!'

'Go to sleep, Lakshmi. I'm going to sleep as well. I'm very tired.'

'Ma, please, play for some time.'

'Please don't nag. I've entertained you long enough. Go on now.'

'Dimma, please tell Ma to play with me. I don't want to sleep.'

'Malati, why don't you play one game and then Lakshmi will be a good girl, right?'

'Ma, please don't force these things on me. You play with her.'

'No, no, no, I will not play with Dimma. I will play with you, Ma,' Lakshmi kept on in a monotone that usually worked with Saraju but always put Malati off.

The little girl brought out her Ludo board, the dice and the counters, hoping that her mother would finally give in.

But Malati's patience had run out. She pushed Lakshmi away with one hand and with the other scattered the pieces of the Ludo board. As she raised her hand to Lakshmi, Saraju intervened.

'I will not let you beat her, Malati. Poor child, all she wanted was to play with her mother, is that so wrong? God is watching you, be careful,' Saraju said sharply. Malati dropped her hand and turned away. Lakshmi sat down to collect the scattered pieces.

Lakshmi admired her mother despite all the cold shouldering she got in return. She watched her in fascination, soaking in everything she did, from the different hairdos she sported, to the way she used kajal, lipstick and powder. She found her mother beautiful and wanted to learn to dress like her. And despite her grandmother's unwavering affection, it was her mother's love that Lakshmi yearned for.

◆

Despite the protective web that Saraju wove around Lakshmi, she was not completely sheltered from the world of flesh that surrounded her. Her first brush with a client happened when she was just nine years old.

Lakshmi had started going to the Corporation-run primary school. But one day, the school sent the children home because a bandh had been declared. The students were given their breakfast and asked to go home. Lakshmi and a group of the neighbourhood children chatted outside the gates of the school for a while and then walked back home.

When Lakshmi got home, the front door was shut but not locked. Lakshmi pushed it open and entered. The house was quiet, so she assumed that Saraju had gone to the bazaar. The door of the bedroom inside was shut. Lakshmi thought that her mother must be with a client. Taking care not to make any noise, she changed into her home clothes and was about to go sit on the porch when she heard heated voices inside the other room. She immediately recognized one of them as her grandmother's. So it was not Malati but Saraju who was with a client! Saraju got customers very rarely these days.

'You drunk fool, let me go. See how you've bruised me, you bastard!' Saraju shouted and ran out of the room, holding her sari around her.

'You old hag…I've paid. You're getting too weak in your old age.'

A middle-aged man came out after her, pulling at her clothes and laughing madly. Lakshmi was stunned but she recovered immediately and instinctively stepped in to help her grandmother.

'Lakshmi, what are you doing here?' Saraju stopped, surprised.

The drunk man had also seen Lakshmi. 'Arre! Who are you, my raw tamarind! Tchhk…!' the man made an obscene slurping sound. His eyes were bloodshot and he was off balance. He was obviously drunk. The huge man charged at Lakshmi.

'Don't you dare, you bastard. Get away from the child,' Saraju screamed, managing to wrap the sari around herself and stand in his way.

'She's mine now! Get out of my way, you shrivelled old nut, or I'll punch your face in.'

'She is still a child…do you understand? A child! We didn't make her "sit" yet and we don't intend to either! We send her to school!'

'Don't worry, I will break her in. How much money do you need, Saraju?' he thundered.

'You will not touch her! Leave right now or I will raise an alarm. Start screaming, Lakshmi!' Saraju started towards the door. Alarm calls worked in Sonagachi. The women looked out for each other.

'Quote anything and I will pay!' he insisted.

Lakshmi did not open the door or call for help. Instead she picked up the umbrella that was lying next to the door, and struck the man on his head with all her might. He fell to the floor with a thud. Blood started slowly oozing from the wound…

Saraju froze for a few minutes. Then she shook herself, but was trembling with fear and rage. The man was an ex-police constable and a long-time client of hers. She was terrified that Lakshmi had killed him.

Lakshmi cried miserably, clinging to Saraju.

'What will happen now, Dimma?'

'It'll be fine, it will all be fine,' Saraju comforted the frightened child. Let me go, stand in that corner. I have to check if he's still breathing,' Saraju whispered. She bolted the front door. The man was breathing. Saraju frantically sprinkled cold water on the man's face in an effort to revive him. Slowly, he groaned and started moving. Finally he opened his eyes. 'Abani babu, please wake up,' Saraju pleaded, now relieved that he was alive.

'Ahh!' he sat up slowly.

Saraju brought a wet cloth to his forehead and then bandaged the wound, all the while talking sweetly to the man in an effort to placate him. She feared that once he recovered and realized that a small child had knocked him out, he would take his revenge on all of them. What if he had them arrested?

'Just lean back here, let me take care of that.'

He was dazed and in pain and the wound was bleeding profusely. Saraju cleaned his wound with Dettol and put lime paste on it to stop the bleeding.

The man finally got up. He no longer looked intoxicated.

'Saraju, I shall not forget this,' he murmured 'How long will you save this slip of a girl?' he said menacingly. He left the room in a huff.

Saraju clasped Lakshmi to her, trying to calm her down. How long would she be able to keep the child safe?

◆

In Sonagachi, fathers did not matter so much and the absence of a father figure in her life did not leave Lakshmi wanting. But she was curious about her father. She would ask Saraju about him. When she saw Malati going out with a man, she would ask Saraju if that was her father. 'Choose the one you like best,' Saraju would joke.

'Should I ask the one whom I like?'

'No, no. You shouldn't. It's a secret you have to find out on your own,' Saraju would say.

One day, sensing that her mother was in a good mood, Lakshmi asked her.

'Ma, was my father good-looking?'
'Why?'
'I just wanted to know.'
'I don't know, but he looked like you.'
'Dimma says I am good-looking.'
'Then go and ask her.'
'Did Dimma know my father?'
'Stop asking stupid questions.'
'Ma, are you angry with him?'
'Why should I be?'
'Because he left us.'
'He didn't leave us. He is dead.'

Malati preferred to think that he was dead, so that is the story she told Lakshmi. Malati was sure that the father was the handsome young man who used to come with Joy sometimes. Lakshmi resembled him. He was a medical student at the R. G. Kar Hospital. He had first come with his friend, Joy. But later he had started coming on his own to see Malati often. Then he stopped coming. Joy told Malati that he had left for England to study. He never came back, never came to know that he had fathered a child.

Over the years, not getting a clear answer, Lakshmi stopped asking about her father.

◆

When Lakshmi was about ten or eleven, Malati took up with Pranay babu. He was a widower with three children and worked as a clerk for one of the erstwhile zamindars who lived near Sovabazar. He was a steady influence in Malati's life, a father figure to Lakshmi and was kind to Saraju. He often told Malati that he wanted to marry her and take her and Lakshmi away from this life. For a while, Malati nursed the dream that he would marry her so that she could take care of his children, while he took care of her daughter and mother.

Of course, that could not happen right away because he depended on his parents and elder brothers for the care of his children. In any case, how would they allow him to take a prostitute for a wife? What would that cost him in society? She knew that this dream might never come to be, but it brought her joy.

For those few years, Malati turned domestic, hardly taking on any other customers. Pranay babu gave her money every month that helped run the household. Even Saraju was surprised to see how Malati softened when her babu was around. He seemed decent and caring and treated Malati like a friend and companion. He did not demand sex the moment he came. Instead, he would bring kochuri-aloordom for all of them, chat and spend time with them. Malati was content with this family. Then, one day, Pranay didn't turn up when he was expected.

Malati didn't think much of this at first—perhaps some work had come up. But as the days passed and neither Pranay nor any word came, Malati started worrying. She had been refusing other clients, getting dressed and waiting for him.

One day, while Malati was waiting for Pranay babu to turn up, Lakshmi realized that her mother was free.

'Ma, will you teach me? I have homework,' Lakshmi said coming out to the veranda. She was dragging her school bag along.

'Lakshmi, sit down here and do it yourself,' Malati said, one eye on the lane below. Her babu would definitely show up today, she thought.

'Ma, we had to draw a wild animal in class today, see, I drew a tiger,' Lakshmi said excitedly, pulling out her drawing book from the bag. Getting no response from Malati, she started tapping her on the shoulder.

'Ma, Ma, look here. Look at my tiger!'

Malati gave the book a cursory glance and looked away.

'Ma, how does it look?' Lakshmi went on. Malati was clearly distracted but little Lakshmi would just not have it.

'Lakshmi, go play with your friends or draw quietly,' Malati said, trying to get Lakshmi to shut up.

'Ma, will you please plait my hair? Dimma has bought me a new ribbon,' Lakshmi carried on, hoping that the change of topic would get her mother's attention. She went in and brought a comb, a bottle of hair oil and the new ribbon and sat down excitedly beside her mother.

'Ma, please oil my hair and comb it. Then plait my hair and tie this ribbon like a butterfly…'

'Later, Lakshmi. Please be quiet now. I'm not feeling well.'

'What happened, Ma, do you have a headache? Should I press your forehead?'

'No, no, just sit quietly. That's it.'

'Ma, look at this ribbon! I wanted a pink one but Dimma got me red…' Lakshmi tried to turn Malati's face towards her. Malati got so thoroughly irritated that she slapped Lakshmi hard.

'Shut up, you bastard, I'll kill you!' Malati shouted loud enough to bring Saraju out. Lakshmi was holding her cheek in shock. Slowly the tears started flowing and then she was howling with rage and pain. Saraju gathered up the crying Lakshmi and took her back inside.

Malati had been in a terrible mood for more than a month. Her babu had stopped coming without any word. But when two months had gone by and he still didn't come, Malati got unnerved. She stopped eating and became depressed, refusing to take on customers. She looked like all the life had leached out of her. This worried Saraju because without Malati working, they would not be able to make ends meet. Malati's depression surprised her—her daughter had had very few emotional attachments even as a young girl. She was not the kind to love anyone or take any relationship too seriously. Saraju thought that Malati was too preoccupied with herself to care deeply about anyone else. Initially, Saraju tried to console Malati and reason with her. For once Malati allowed it and did not snap at her mother. But when Malati's depression didn't abate, Saraju sent for Paltu. She wanted him to find out what had happened to Pranay. Saraju was sure that he had just moved on, but Malati wasn't willing to let go.

Paltu had remained in Malati's life, but seeing how she treated her daughter hurt him deeply. He could understand her stand-offish behaviour with him and even forgive her rudeness towards Saraju, but what had the innocent child done? He avoided her, but came by to see Saraju and Lakshmi. The little girl was attached to him and he was very fond of her, and always brought her little gifts. When Saraju asked for his help, he couldn't say no. And seeing Malati in such distress upset him. Malati broke down on seeing Paltu.

'Will you please bring him back, Paltu?' Malati wept.

Malati didn't know her babu's address. She just knew his name and the fact that his house on Creek Row was next to a popular bike mechanic's makeshift shack.

'I will try but I don't know if I'll be able to find him and even if I do, will he even talk to me?' Paltu tried to reason with Malati.

'Just bring him to me once, Paltu. I have to know what happened.' Malati told him that she feared that her babu had died. Perhaps her pride couldn't handle the fact that the man who had been offering her marriage and companionship would just stop showing up.

'I'll try my best,' Paltu's voice shook, but Malati was too engulfed in her grief to notice that.

Paltu wasn't keen on going because he knew that no babu who was a regular at Sonagachi ever wanted his mistress to send word or a messenger home. That is the reason addresses were never shared. But he couldn't say no to Malati.

Paltu did find the man with some difficulty. He had remarried and was living with his new wife. He came out of the house to meet Paltu whom he recognized from Sonagachi.

'How did you find me?' he asked in shock, as he took Paltu aside.

'Malati is heartbroken. She wants to know what happened to you,' Paltu explained.

'I'm married now. I'm sure she understands that this was not a permanent arrangement. I don't owe her anything.' He shoved a few notes into Paltu's hands.

'No, she doesn't. Malati is in a bad shape. She cries all day, worried about you, thinking you might be dead…' Paltu insisted.

'You have your story right there. Go and tell her that I died in an accident. Keep my secret and I'll give you some money when I can. You can find me at the Bagbazar Ghat every Sunday.' Pranay babu had been worried that Malati would find out about his broken promises and create a scene. He knew how volatile she could be. Now he could use Paltu to make sure that didn't happen. Paltu felt a surge of hatred for the man. He was no different from the hundreds of men who came to Sonagachi every day, why did Malati think he was special? Paltu didn't reply; he took the money, turned and left in disgust.

After returning to Sonagachi, Paltu carefully broke the news of Pranay's death to Malati and left her to cope with her grief. He went back the next morning and at her insistence took her to a local ghat on the banks of the Ganges to perform the funeral rites. Malati took off her sindoor, shankha-pola, the symbols of a Bengali married woman that she had started wearing with Pranay and never wore red again.

6.

Ever since Malati was young, she loved being photographed. She would get dressed, dress up Lakshmi and drag Golapi and Prateek to the photo studio every time she felt like getting photographs taken. Very often, Saraju would also accompany them. She collected these photographs in albums. Malati loved to pore over these photographs and ruminate. Sometimes when her mother was away and Saraju was busy, or when it was raining and she had nothing else to do, Lakshmi would take out those treasured albums and leaf through them. There was a family photograph of Saraju, Malati and four-year-old Lakshmi in Saraju's arms. All three of them wore kajal and lipstick, which was apparent even in the black-and-white photograph. There was another photograph of Golapi and Prateek. He looked to be around six years old. Golapi and Prateek had been a part of their lives as long as Lakshmi could remember. Prateek was her playmate and protector, he would stand up for her if any of the other kids tried to bully her. Golapi and Malati had been there for each other through all their ups and downs. Golapi was Malati's only friend.

When Malati found out that Pranay babu had died, Golapi was struggling with her health. She had spent a good part of her youth in Sonamukhi's household but had finally managed to buy her way out and taken up a small rented room three lanes away from her earlier quarters. She had been doing well for herself and had managed to keep the household going. In the past few months, however, she hadn't been able to shake off a fever. It left her tired and often unable to work. She tried to conserve all her strength for her business and stayed indoors the rest of the time. But when Prateek came back one day and told his mother that Malati mashi was crying because she had become a widow, she gathered her strength and went at once to see her friend. She was the only one who knew of the secret dreams that Malati had had about starting a family with her babu. Malati had told Golapi that she was saving money so that she could finally quit the trade and set up home near Bagbazar. And now she had become a widow? How heartbroken she must be!

When Malati opened the door and let her in, the two friends cried in each other's arms. Golapi knew it was her turn to take care of Malati. She took Lakshmi to stay with her for a few days. A change of scene would do her good and give Saraju and Malati some space. Malati refused to take clients for close to three months after this. Golapi brought money and food with her whenever she could, sharing her income with Saraju, who was working as a domestic help in the neighbouring households. Between them, they somehow managed until Malati gradually came around. Finally, Malati asked her pimp to find her clients once again. Saraju was relieved.

But through all this Golapi's illness persisted. She ignored it for as long as she could and tried to keep living a normal life. When it got bad and other symptoms like diarrhoea, nausea, chest pain, dryness of the mouth and mouth ulcers became unbearable, she went to the local doctor who gave her some generic painkillers and antibiotics. That contained the illness for some time, but it came back again and again. For nearly two years, Golapi lived with the disease and ultimately succumbed to a combination of hepatitis and venereal diseases. Malati was overwhelmed with grief. She had lost a sister, her closest confidante, someone whom she loved more than her babu, her daughter and her mother.

But the person who was most affected by Golapi's death was her son. Prateek's world crashed. Malati, Saraju and Paltu tried to help him as much as possible. They insisted that he stay with them, fed him and tried to convince him to stay in school. But after the initial shock wore off, Prateek felt more comfortable in his own home. He started working for the brothel owners and began bringing customers for the women in the brothels. The men would hand over a tip and the brothel owners paid him a small amount. The boy just about stayed afloat, missing his mother dearly at every step. Prateek managed for a while. And then his life changed in ways he could have never imagined.

A few months after Golapi had died, a social worker from a local NGO visited his house. The volunteer, Teresa, a foreigner, was trying to spread awareness about the use of condoms in Sonagachi.

'Hi! I'm Teresa, what's your name?' a woman stood there beaming at Prateek. She was dressed in a simple salwar kameez.

'Prateek,' he answered, wide-eyed.

Teresa now switched to Bengali. 'Can you call your mother and the other women of the house, please? I need to talk to them,' she said. All volunteers needed to learn Bengali and Hindi to be able to work in Sonagachi.

'No one else is here,' Prateek answered.

'Where's your mother?' Teresa asked.

'She's dead.'

'So who takes care of you?'

'My mother's friends. I also work for the mashis and make some money.'

'But you can't live like this!'

'I can take care of myself.' Prateek looked at Teresa defiantly, but his voice quivered.

Teresa was a British student who worked with Hope for Life. She was in Kolkata for a year, volunteering with Durjoy, the Indian partner of Hope for Life. Durjoy focused on spreading health awareness in red-light areas.

Teresa brought up Prateek's case to Swadesh Dey, the chief of Durjoy and a doctor. 'He's too young to be left on his own. He could get sexually exploited and I'm not sure he's even eating properly or bathing regularly.'

The doctor knew Golapi. 'His mother died of hepatitis. She came to me in the last hour. The battle was already lost by then. You don't need money to get yourself treated here but most girls avoid us…' Swadesh said.

'What can we do for her son?' Teresa was concerned.

Swadesh hated losing a patient, even when he knew there was nothing he could have done. Having failed Golapi, he was determined to help her son. Durjoy ran a home for orphaned children of Sonagachi. They also put up the children for adoption.

'Let's get him into the orphanage. He can live there and continue his studies. Perhaps one day, he can also become our liaison between the NGO and the sex workers,' the doctor said.

Prateek was enrolled in the orphanage. He went back to school. The doctor also got him involved in the daily workings of the NGO and he started learning the ropes. While he was officially meant to live at the orphanage, as he spent so much time at the NGO office, he ended up living with the doctor and his wife whose residence was on the second floor of the Durjoy office. The couple treated the young boy like their own. Prateek returned the love in full measure.

While he was an all-round assistant and helped with every aspect of the NGO, the work that truly called to him was the health awareness programme. Over the years, he learnt more about the diseases that killed his mother and the many sex workers who were affected by them. He began helping the volunteers organize health awareness camps. Durjoy had been facing a lot of resistance from the prostitutes as well as their customers for trying to push the use of condoms. The brothel owners and the girls themselves knew that they would lose customers if they insisted on condoms. Though he was slightly underage, Prateek helped Durjoy's doctors and volunteers go from room to room talking to the girls and explaining to them that unprotected sex exposed them to killer diseases. Prateek became a symbol—the orphan who had lost his sex worker mother to a sexually transmitted disease.

Prateek was the youngest member of the team, but Dr Dey started giving him more and more responsibilities. In time, Prateek became a key person for Durjoy. He liaised with the media on the one hand and volunteers from foreign NGOs on the other. Dr Dey designed a unique campaign for the rights of the women in the sex trade and this drew a lot of media attention. Prateek had managed to get some of the women to participate. He had taken their suggestions and included them in the campaign. Slogans were raised, walls were filled with graffiti, posters and banners were printed and both the print and TV media lapped up all that Durjoy had to show. The presence of a plethora of foreign volunteers was an added attraction. Prateek was a prominent face of this campaign.

◆

Saraju struggled up the stairs to her house. She had to stop to catch her breath every couple of steps, she felt a sharp pain in her chest. She had always been healthy. But her life had been difficult and full of hard physical labour that had sapped her vitality. All these years, she had managed to do the work that was needed with no complaints. In recent years, she had been working as a housemaid in the neighbourhood. But in the past few months, even the lightest housework was proving to be too much for her. She was losing weight steadily. Lakshmi insisted on taking her to the doctor. There was no apparent ailment, no fever, cold and cough, stomach disorders. But the doctor diagnosed that she had suffered from years of overwork, malnutrition and stress. The only prescription was nutritious food and complete rest. This meant that she could not keep working as a housemaid—the cleaning and cooking was too hard on her. This put a financial strain on the household. It was understood that sooner rather than later, Lakshmi would have to be inducted into the business.

Saraju was adamantly against this. She had often suggested to Malati that they get Lakshmi married off to Prateek—she knew he was a good boy and with his recent success at the NGO, he would be able to care for her. But as Prateek collected success and accolades, Lakshmi felt that he was no longer a part of her world. When she saw him these days, he was with the volunteers of the

NGO, telling the women of Sonagachi about right and wrong. Over the past few years, their relationship had strained. She no longer thought of Prateek as her closest friend. Prateek didn't throw his weight around with Saraju's family, but Lakshmi was convinced that he thought too highly of himself.

Prateek, the poster boy of Durjoy, was awarded by the social welfare ministry for his work in building a vigilance team of retired sex workers to stop human trafficking. He donated his prize money of five lakh rupees to Durjoy—he wanted to give back to the organization that had given him so much. It was to be utilized to educate the children of prostitutes. The NGO was delighted and the local media swarmed him—his story was moving.

Lakshmi saw this and felt a stab of jealousy. Never a diligent student, since her grandmother had fallen ill, Lakshmi had hardly been attending school. She didn't give the final exams for Class VIII. Saraju was devastated. She could see that Malati was getting ready to induct Lakshmi. Lakshmi saw it as well—she had nursed the hope that her life might be different. But now, that was no longer possible. Every time Prateek was mentioned or she saw his photo in the newspapers, she realized how great the gulf between them had grown. She had been avoiding him, but he caught up with her one day.

'Lakshmi! Why didn't you come to the meeting today? I didn't see Malati mashi either!' Prateek asked. Lakshmi was setting off from home and Prateek came running after her. Durjoy had held an open meeting where volunteers and doctors met sex workers, exchanged information and set up counselling appointments. Malati and Lakshmi were meant to attend.

'I couldn't. Dimma is not well,' Lakshmi said shortly. She had stepped out of the house to go to the market.

'What happened?'

'The usual. Fever...weakness.'

'Where are you going?'

'To buy medicines.'

'I'll come with you. I haven't seen you in a while,' Prateek started walking with Lakshmi.

'Prateek, leave me alone. I'm not in the mood to talk to you.'

'Are you angry with me, Lakshmi?'

'Angry? Are you really interested in what I'm feeling? You come and go as you please and why not! You're a big guy here, who am I?'

'I keep coming back to you, Lakshmi, but you never seem to respond.'

'You don't have time for people like me, Prateek. Dimma is ill, money is tight. I've not been going to school...and my mother will want me to start working soon,' Lakshmi walked away, trying to stifle her tears.

Prateek stopped in his tracks and stood staring as Lakshmi disappeared down the road.

He no longer thought that he and Lakshmi would get married, but he was devastated that she seemed to hate him now. Every time they had such fights Prateek would promise never to bother Lakshmi again, but invariably he would find his way back to her.

A few days after this, Lakshmi woke in the morning to find her grandmother dead beside her. At first, Lakshmi was surprised that Saraju was still in bed—she was an early riser and would bathe, wash her clothes and complete her puja before the others woke up. Lakshmi nudged her. Saraju was unnaturally stiff and cold. Lakshmi sat up and touched her grandmother's cheeks and hands. They were cold as ice.

Lakshmi shouted, 'Ma! Dimma nei!' tears were streaming down her face.

Malati, still groggy, came out of her room. 'What happened? Why are you screaming?' she asked.

'Dimma's dead!' Lakshmi managed to blurt out, seized by sobs.

Malati walked towards her mother. It was clear that she had died some hours ago.

Lakshmi sat on the floor by the bed and broke down. She felt a physical pain. Malati didn't cry but sat still at the foot of the bed for a long while, staring blankly. Then she got up to find Paltu.

◆

'Don't take Dimma away... Dimma...Dimma...' Lakshmi wailed as Prateek, Paltu and the neighbours prepared the body and got ready to take Saraju to the ghat for the final rites. Sonamukhi, Bula, Shefali and many of the women who had known Saraju came to pay their last respects. Sonamukhi hugged Malati, 'Your mother was a strong woman. She will want you to be strong for yourself and for her beloved granddaughter.' She wiped away her tears and hobbled down the stairs, helped by two of the girls from her brothel.

Lakshmi sat back on the floor and cried silently. She felt lost and alone. After the neighbours had left, Malati roused Lakshmi out of her stupor. 'Let's wash everything and clean the house. This is mandatory after a death. You have to let fresh air in,' Malati said.

Together they collected all the sheets and their clothes in buckets, locked the door and went to the tap. Seeing them, others made way. Sonagachi respected bereavements. They came back home and hung up the wet sheets and clothes to dry. Malati and Lakshmi worked quietly. They didn't speak about Saraju but they were both thinking about the woman who had been their pillar of strength, working to keep the family together.

For the rest of the day, Malati and Lakshmi sat around, doing nothing and speaking very little. Both Paltu and Prateek checked on them through the day and brought them food. But neither of them ate. The next day, Paltu brought tea and biscuits early in the morning. Another day without Dimma, Lakshmi thought. As far back as she could remember, Lakshmi had always seen herself as part of a threesome. Her grandmother had been the one who nurtured her and fought for her, protected her from the world, even from her own mother. She didn't know how to live without her guiding light.

A few days later, Lakshmi was still moving around in a daze. At times during the day, she would be overwhelmed with memories of her grandmother and break down. But Malati soon ran out of patience. She had to start working to keep the household functioning. 'Stop brooding and get up now. You have to help me with the work,' Malati chided Lakshmi.

Paltu had walked in with two packets of puri-sabji.

'Get up, wash up. Eat what Paltu has brought and let's start work.'

Paltu could see that Lakshmi was still fragile, so he stepped in. 'Lakshmi, darling, Dimma hasn't gone anywhere, she's watching you from above and blessing you,' he said kindly. 'You will feel her around you, and she will shower you with her blessings to keep you safe and happy,' he said.

When Lakshmi stepped out to go to the common bathroom, Paltu softly admonished Malati, 'Just be a little more patient with the girl, Malati. It's been a big loss to her.'

'Do you think it's not a loss to me? The girl has to get stronger. It's time she started bringing in some money,' Malati said.

'Earning? She is too young, Malati. How can you do this to your own daughter! You didn't bring her up with this idea.' This was the point on which he and Saraju had always been united, much to Malati's disgust. She had always told them it was foolish for them to have big dreams for Lakshmi and give her false hope.

'What do you expect me to do with her?'

'Not what you do, certainly!'

'And what's wrong with what I do? Am I not earning my living honestly?'

'I didn't mean that, Malati, and you know that well. God knows I am a beneficiary too—'

They cut the conversation short when they heard Lakshmi coming back.

Lakshmi had been very erratic with school in the past few months when she had been taking care of her grandmother. Now she stopped going at all and began taking on most of the work at home. Malati hated household chores and was relieved that Lakshmi had taken over the housework with minimum fuss. She didn't force Lakshmi to start taking on customers…yet. She knew that Lakshmi could not be kept out of the trade for too long. She didn't discuss her doubts with anyone, but she battled with herself over the idea.

Lakshmi had grown into a lovely young girl. After that scary encounter with Saraju's client when she was young, there had been many instances when Malati's customers started asking about her. Some of them would become insistent and offer money. Malati was worried that she could not put them off much longer, now that Saraju was also not around. She asked Paltu to stand guard at times. He had even started sleeping in the veranda at night, something that Lakshmi appreciated greatly. He had always been kind to her, nurtured her and was a constant father figure. He had pulled away from Malati for a while. But after Saraju's death, Malati began relying on him a lot more.

One night, an agitated conversation inside her mother's room woke Lakshmi. She was surprised because Malati hadn't said anything about taking on a customer that late. As she listened, Lakshmi recognized Paltu's voice and couldn't resist eavesdropping. She tiptoed to the door and stood there listening.

'Now that you don't sleep in your room, why don't we use it for Lakshmi so that she can start her own business?' Malati said.

'Let her go back to school, Malati. Don't introduce her just as yet, she's just a kid, let's spare her this life,' Paltu pleaded.

'She's going to be fifteen soon and should start sitting. I have already spoken to Suhani to train Lakshmi. Suhani will charge, of course, and I will pay some money. Lakshmi can pay the rest when she starts earning.'

'Can we not get her married?'

'Who will marry a prostitute's daughter?'

'What about Prateek?'

'Prateek has been able to extricate himself from this business. These days he lives with the sahibs at their office, studies and lives an upper-class life like the bhadra babus. Let us not dream but do what's best for Lakshmi and us,' Malati said, her voice harsh.

'Yes, his life has changed, but he still keeps in touch with all of us. He is being trained to fight for the rights of the girls here,' Paltu insisted.

'Let him try. Nothing will ever change in Sonagachi,' Malati said bitterly.

'You just don't want to give up the money that your daughter will earn. You are a greedy woman,' Paltu said.

'Shut up, you soft old fool!' Malati hissed. 'She's my daughter and I will decide what needs to be done with her,' Malati growled.

'She's my daughter too!' Paltu said quietly.

'Says who? Not even Lakshmi herself thinks so!'

The fact that her mother wanted her to sit was not much of a surprise, but hearing that she had started preparing for her training was a bit of a shock. Even worse was how her mother belittled Paltu. She ran back to her bed and threw herself down, burying her face in the pillow.

Lakshmi woke up early the next day. She saw Paltu sitting in the slice of sunlight in the veranda. He was sitting hunched, smoking a beedi. She got up quietly from the bed and sat down beside him, and put her head on his shoulder. He put his frail, protective arm around her. They both sat silently for a while as the sun came up and the lanes started bustling around them.

BOOK II

# 7.

Paul and Zoya Smith got down from the cab at the gates of St John's Church and walked in. Zoya had been sick the day after they landed. But rest and some sleep had done wonders. After a light breakfast at their hotel, the couple had set off to the church to meet Father Julius. Paul, a documentary filmmaker, had met Father Julius many years ago when he had been working with Hope for Life in London. Paul had a connection to the city—his great-grandparents had lived in Calcutta during the years of the Raj. Ever since Paul had discovered the photo albums, letters and other memorabilia from this period in his family home, he had been consumed by their lives. He longed to connect with this part of his family's history.

Baron Charles Smith had set up one of England's first cotton textile mills in Birmingham. A successful businessman, he had travelled to India as part of the East India Company and traded for the cotton that was used to make the yarn and cloth in his mills. Smith's youngest son, William, followed in his father's footsteps, joining the British East India Company and then the British government. William spent most of his time in India in Calcutta. He was Paul's great-grandfather. Paul had heard some of the stories about William being born in a haveli in Calcutta and his friendship with the local raja.

Once Paul discovered the photographs, letters and diaries, he found out more about his ancestors and about the Calcutta of that period. From the photographs, it was clear that the haveli where they had lived for generations was beautiful—it had ornate pillars, Belgian glass chandeliers, coloured glass windows and frescoes that depicted scenes from the Hindu epics. Originally a raja's palace, the Smiths had lived there, paying nominal rent until Independence.

Paul had sent these descriptions as well as a photograph that showed the entrance to the palace to Father Julius. There were pillars on either side of the gate with marble plaques on the base. The one on the left read 'Singha Palace' while the one on the right read 'Raja Gourmohan Singha'. The pillars were in the shape of roaring lions wearing crowns and holding sceptres.

Father Julius had recognized the palace from this photo and had promised to take Paul there when he visited. It was only now, many years later that Paul had managed to make the trip to Calcutta.

Paul and Zoya climbed the flight of stairs that led to the massive prayer hall with hundreds of wooden pews leading to the altar; they heard music from a pipe organ. As they got closer to the music, they saw the massive pipe organ. Instruments such as these are not seen any more because they are very hard to maintain. The pipe organ hardly looked like a musical instrument but rather like a small wooden room with scores of metal pipes reaching up to the ceiling. Zoya gasped.

'I didn't imagine anything like this could exist outside English churches!'

As they drew closer, they saw a middle-aged cassock-clad

priest playing the instrument, his fingers flying over the keys. Two young men stood next to him, with tools in their hands. The atmosphere in the church was charged; it felt like they could have been in another time and place. The priest had his eyes closed as he played 'He is My Everything' and the entire prayer hall reverberated with the soulful tune. When he finally finished the piece, Paul and Zoya clapped enthusiastically.

Father Julius looked up in surprise and then broke into a smile. Nearly six feet tall, he was lithe and handsome. 'Paul, Zoya, welcome,' he said, standing up to greet them. 'I wanted to get the work on the pipe organ started. These young men have come from Chennai to restore it. You know, it was installed here by none other than Warren Hastings!'

'Very few instruments that old would be in working condition, Father!' said Paul.

'This one had stopped working many years ago. You will be surprised to see how mammoth the instrument is. Look in this ante-chamber—see how a pump is first used to let air into the pipes, only after that can you start playing the keys,' Father Julius showed them.

Zoya, an enthusiastic student of history, had many questions about the church. Father Julius, a fellow history enthusiast, was only too happy to share.

'St John's was the first Anglican Cathedral built in colonial Calcutta. Warren Hastings, the then governor general, used funds from the East India Company to build it. It was modelled on St Martin-in-the-Fields in Trafalgar Square, London. So it's not surprising that it feels like home to you,' Father Julius said. He then took them around the different chambers of the massive church. The building had been constructed using a combination of bricks and stones. This had led to its local sobriquet: Pathure Girja. Then they went into the vast gardens that housed the tomb of Job Charnock, the famed East India Company trader who landed on the eastern bank of the Hooghly and kick-started the British colonization of India.

'Come, let's have lunch,' Father Julius said and led them to his residence at the northeast corner of the garden. A gravel path ran down the middle of the garden and led to a portico of the two-storeyed house. Although the Anglican Church allowed priests to marry, Father Julius had remained single. The house that served as the residence of the parish priest was ancient but its interiors were modern and comfortable. Father Julius had asked the cook to serve Bengali side dishes with rice. Paul and Zoya ate enthusiastically, using their fingers, guided all the while by Father Julius. They chatted as they ate, catching up on all the news. Then, as they had planned, they set off for Singha Palace.

The drive to Sovabazar, just five kilometres away, took them nearly forty minutes despite the lean afternoon traffic. Father Julius gave instructions to the driver in Bengali before they drove off. The crowd seemed to swell as the car crossed the Esplanade and moved northwards. Zoya tried to read signboards on the old mansions that lined both sides of Chittaranjan Avenue. These mammoth buildings were crowded with residents and clothes were drying on nearly every grilled veranda. Most of the buildings looked run down.

'I've imagined this mansion based on stories that my grandmother told me. She had heard about it from her mother-in-law…it's nostalgia, romance and magic all rolled into one, Father,' Paul said emotionally.

'I know. But I'm afraid what you will see won't match that romance. I hope you won't be too disappointed. The house is rather dilapidated.'

They parked the car in the lane and got off. Old, once-palatial buildings lined the street on both sides. Paul stood there looking around with the curiosity of a child. None of these buildings looked like the one he had seen in the photograph. Could it have changed completely? But if that was the case, then Father Julius would not have been able to locate it. Paul waited while Father Julius gave the driver some instructions.

The signboards told them that they were on Raja Gourmohan Singha Street. Old double-storeyed buildings supported by ornate pillars and columns stood out against the modern buildings on the adjacent streets. None of the buildings were well maintained. Their white exteriors were damaged, the plaster had broken off, exposing the underlying bricks. Deep cracks had developed all over the walls. In many places, the cornices had fallen off. Father Julius told them about the area as they walked in a single file, negotiating cars, bikes and bicycles.

'This is the oldest part of Kolkata. It was developed by Raja Gourmohan Singha, a zamindar who allied with Lord Clive. He was awarded the title of raja for the help he gave Clive. All the palatial houses in the row belonged to his family and continue to do so to this day.'

Soon they reached the Sovabazar Rajbari, Gourmohan Singha's main palace. It was a sprawling complex with a courtyard in the middle and living quarters around it. The lime white of the palace shone in the blazing sun.

'This building has received some state funding,' Father Julius explained. 'That's why it's better maintained. Father Julius led them through the courtyard.

'This covered space is called the thakurdalan. Gourmohan's famed Durga Puja was held here in the presence of Clive.' They continued to the rear end of the palace, crossed a garden of tall fruit trees and reached a small clearing near the boundary wall. They crossed the tall gate to enter another mansion.

Father Julius drew their attention to the remnants of two pillars that were on either side of a gate. He then asked Paul to examine the marble slab and moved aside the creepers that had grown over it.

'Look closely. What do you see?''

'Umm… Singha Palace! This is it!' Paul exclaimed, his voice rising in excitement.

'Let me see,' Zoya pushed her way to the slab.

'Yes, I can see how it used to look. In the photos the lions on the pillars were intact and the marble slab clear…but there's no mistaking it,' Paul said.

Father Julius led them in. 'The property still belongs to the raja's family. When your great-grandfather lived here as special assistant to the governor general, the house was reserved for Company use. The land on which my church stands was also donated to the Company by Raja Gourmohan Singha.'

As they neared the door, two men dressed in khaki shirts and dhotis came up and saluted the priest. He spoke to them in Bengali and they ran ahead of the group to open the rickety main door.

'Of course, no one lives here anymore. Parts of the masonry fall off every now and then. Real estate promoters would love to buy the land and build a new apartment block here. But the property is under litigation, so selling it is impossible,' Father Julius continued.

They walked into the two-storeyed building. After crossing a big hall, they came to a veranda that ran along the entire quadrangular structure. The rooms opened onto this veranda. The layout was more or less the same on the first floor. The two workers brought the party to the central courtyard. A big flight of stairs rose at one end of the courtyard.

'There is a dance floor somewhere upstairs. It's called Nautch Ghar—I've seen it in one of the photographs,' Paul said, walking towards the stairs. The two caretakers protested. Father Julius explained.

'The staircase is not safe, Paul. Take it easy, you have enough time to explore slowly.'

Father Julius told the caretakers that Paul would come back again and requested them to help him if they could.

◆

Paul and Zoya were following Father Julius through the narrow lanes of Sonagachi. It was 6.30 p.m. and, after a satisfying visit to the Singha Palace, Father Julius had asked the couple if they would mind going with him to Sonagachi—Kolkata's oldest and biggest sex district. The priest was the point person for Hope for Life and its collaborations with NGOs in the area and wanted to meet someone with regard to that. Singha Palace and its environs had clearly seen better days, but nothing about the red-light district seemed to have been good at any time. The lanes were narrow, the whole area smelled bad, water was puddled in low-lying areas. Paul and Zoya were shocked.

'I don't believe what I'm seeing, Zoya! I have seen so many films on prostitution and the flesh chain that extends from countries like India, Bangladesh, Pakistan and Afghanistan to the Middle East. But nothing had prepared me for this!' a shocked Paul said.

Zoya held her scarf over her nose to avoid the appalling stench. She knew it was rude, but couldn't help herself. Young children played on the streets and men and women went about their lives seemingly without even being aware of the smells.

Father Julius seemed at home in these lanes. After lunch, he had changed from his cassock to a half-sleeved shirt and trousers and was wearing covered rubber shoes. He had asked Paul and Zoya to change to such shoes. People shouted out greetings to Father Julius and a few stopped to chat with him. He smiled and spoke to each of them.

'What a drastic change from the rest of the city, isn't it?' Zoya asked, trying to ward off the swarms of flies as they negotiated the dingy lanes made narrower because of the piles of garbage and dirt and clothes hanging on clotheslines outside the quarters. Narrow lanes crisscrossed like a maze. On both sides of these lanes stood shanties—damp and shabby looking grey buildings of various heights that housed the prostitutes' quarters. They stood so close to each other that they appeared to guard against sunlight, making sure none of it passed through.

The evening was the prime time for women to attract customers, so they stood outside, trying their best to get the attention of passers-by. Some wore saris, others were in cotton gowns while the youngest girls wore jeans and tops—all in loud colours, covering little. As potential customers walked by, the women preened and tried to show off their assets, pouted, bit their lips and gave them their best come-hither looks. Those who had managed to bait customers stood apart and haggled in soft voices. Those who didn't sometimes swore or passed lewd comments before moving on to the next customer.

Young children stood with some of the women, playing games. Zoya's heart went out to the children. She wondered who cared for them while their mothers were working. She was thankful when they finally reached the NGO's modest office. It was clean and had an air freshener. There was no air conditioner but the ceiling fans sufficed. Zoya noticed that there were several rooms in this one-storey building and there were children in these rooms. There were cartoons and cut-outs of animals on the chart papers and colourful posters on the soft boards, indicating that the place was used for children.

Tea arrived on a tray. Tea with milk and sugar. On their outing today, Paul and Zoya had been fascinated by the small tea stalls that dotted the city and the tiny terracotta cups in which cha was served. They had planned on trying that tea very soon.

Now, as Father Julius handed the paper cups to Paul and Zoya, they eagerly took them and sipped with relish.

'Robert and his wife, Martha, both from Scotland, will soon be here. They are child educators and are on a social service holiday sponsored by the British Council. They had applied to Hope for Life and were assigned work here,' Father Julius said.

'How long have they been here?' Zoya asked.

'It's been six months now and they have done some wonderful work on English phonics with these children, Zoya,' Father Julius said.

'Where do they stay?' Zoya asked.

'They have taken up rented rooms at Sovabazar. Paul, I am sure you understand now that we are not very far from your Singha Palace. It is this proximity that made it possible for me to locate the building, because in all these years I have become familiar with this place,' Father Julius said.

As they were talking, Robert and Martha walked in. The four volunteers were happy to see each other and soon started talking about the work they could do here. Paul and Zoya wondered how best they could help.

'Oh, you are most welcome to join us. I'm sure Prateek would love it. What do you think, Father?' Robert asked.

'Yes, he keeps complaining about the lack of helping hands. He has roped in some local volunteers but they need training. Oh, I have an idea! Paul, why don't you and Zoya train these volunteers! It will be a great help!' Father Julius suggested.

'Certainly. I can do that. But is there a set programme?' Zoya asked.

'Father, I see that there are some teenagers too. Instead of teaching them school subjects, maybe I can teach them photography? That way I will be able to give them something; classroom teaching is really not my forte,' Paul confessed.

'The local civic body runs a school for kids here and we try to supplement this. For the pre-schoolers there is no specific syllabus to follow. We just teach the English alphabet through phonics, rhymes, some drawing and painting. We send the older children to school and follow through with what they learn there. The idea is to prevent drop outs so that they get basic education and stay in a healthy environment for a few hours after school. The aim is to make them employable once they turn eighteen, so that they have options outside the sex business,' Martha explained.

Just then, tall, dark and well-built Prateek walked into the room. He looked serious and much older than his eighteen years.

'Here comes Prateek, our project co-ordinator here. He's extremely hard-working and passionate about the cause. You can seek his help whenever you want and he can take you around and explain things much better than we can,' Robert said.

'Good evening, Father, good evening sirs, good evening ma'ams,' Prateek said, inclining his head.

'So, how's everything, young man? You've not brought any new kids for my school!' Father Julius asked Prateek.

'Father, there are a few boys who are ready for your school. I'm having problems with the girls. There are some who can be taken to the Baptist Mission School, Bowbazar, but in most cases the mothers are unwilling. They need to be counselled. I am trying my best but…' Prateek trailed off. He spoke all the while in English and the newcomers were thoroughly impressed.

'Don't worry, son. I know how hard you try. Meet Paul and Zoya from England. They will come to help out whenever they find time,' Father Julius said.

'That will be great!' Prateek said.

'Though Prateek didn't have formal schooling, his mentor, the chief of Durjoy has trained him. Working with Hope For Life has done the rest. The result is there for everyone to see!' Father Julius said proudly.

Zoya discussed with Martha how she could help. They decided that she would teach the students English, and train the volunteers. Paul had a slightly different plan. Could he tell the story of Sonagachi's women and children, he wondered? The cameras started rolling in his head and he felt a kick of excitement. This film might just be a life-changing story, both for himself and for some of the kids here.

Later that night after dinner, Zoya, Paul and Father Julius discussed Paul's idea. Paul wanted to embed himself in the community and tell the real up, close and personal story of the people there.

'This will be rather difficult in a place like Sonagachi, the priest explained. 'The women in the red-light area are suspicious of people they don't know. They think that society at large hounds them. There was a lot of resistance to Durjoy in the beginning. I suggest you speak to Prateek and see how best you can do this.'

'Is Prateek from Sonagachi?' Zoya asked.

'Yes,' said Father Julius. He then told them how the young man had come to work with Durjoy.

The next day Paul spoke to Prateek to get his input. 'I was toying with an idea, Prateek. I need your help,' Paul said, talking slowly and deliberately so that the young man could understand him.

Prateek, who had come to know that Paul was a filmmaker, was rather excited to be working with him.

'I want to pick a group of six children—boys and girls of different age groups—children whose mothers are sex workers. We'll find the funds to admit them into formal schools. I plan to be here for a year at the least, perhaps two. In that time, we will give the kids a camera each. I will teach them how to use these cameras. When they are with me, we will wander through the city and they can take pictures and videos of anything that they find interesting. I want to follow their lives and help them find work outside of Sonagachi eventually. I want to film this transformation. What do you think?'

Prateek thought this through. It might work. Even if all the children involved could not find their way out of Sonagachi, it would definitely be a life-changing experience. 'I shall find you six boys and girls of varying age groups, sir! I'll help you any way I can,' Prateek said excitedly.

It was not difficult for him to induct some of the younger children into this project. He spoke to the mothers of some of the kids who came to the day care at the NGO. Four of them saw the potential in it and agreed. Paul had mentioned that he would like to have some older children and definitely some girls in the group. Of course, Lakshmi was the first person Prateek thought of. Lakshmi needed the help and God knows how desperately he wanted to be able to do something for her. There was another girl around Lakshmi's age, Keka. Her mother would also not be easily amenable to this kind of thing.

A couple of days later, he had made arrangements with the mothers of the four young boys. Prateek suggested to Paul that he start working with them. 'Sir, their mothers have no problem about them being away the whole day. In fact, they sounded happy that their kids would get a chance to go to an English school…but…' Prateek told Paul.

'But what, Prateek?'

'The problem is with the older girls, Lakshmi and Keka. Lakshmi's mother is on the verge of getting her daughter started in sex work, sir, but I want to try…'

'If she's a problem, let us get someone else…' Paul suggested.

'Sir, Lakshmi is an intelligent girl. I'm sure she'll learn fast. It might be her only chance at a different life,' Prateek said softly, not meeting Paul's eyes.

Paul sensed the urgency in the young man's voice. It was clear that Prateek had more than a cursory interest in Lakshmi. 'Will money work to convince her family?' he suggested.

'Yes!' Prateek sounded relieved. 'That is the only thing that works here, sir!'

'Let me see what I can do,' Paul said thoughtfully.

8.

Zoya paired up with Martha and started visiting the NGO every day to teach the children and train the volunteers. Paul wanted to wait for the full group to come together before he started working with them. In the meantime, he decided to take his camera into the alleys of Sonagachi and do some filming on his own.

But Prateek didn't think this was a good idea. 'Sir, please do not move about on your own. It is not a very good place for visitors.'

'What do you mean?' Paul asked.

'Here, every outsider is a potential client. Whoever is not a client has no business being here!'

'I can't blame them. What wretched lives they lead here…'

'Yes, sir. And there is always some who are being exploited and there is perversion and crime…'

'I won't go out alone, but you can understand that I want to collect material from here that I might be able to use in a film.'

'I agree, sir, but that is where the problem lies. If they see a stranger moving around with a camera, they will think you are a reporter who will only have negative things to say about them and their lives…'

'Hmm…I understand…it's a defence mechanism, Prateek.'

'I'll ask Ganesh, an office assistant at Durjoy, to take you around. His mother is a sex worker in Sonagachi, he knows the place and the people here know him. But please do not take your camera inside any brothel.'

Paul looked up at Prateek, expecting more. Prateek looked uncomfortable but spoke up. 'Sorry about this, sir, but filming pornography had become the rage here these days. The women are eager to pose for stills and allow filming of the act since they get paid well. They demand a higher price for weird poses...so a camera can be dangerous if you are alone...'

Paul could see how embarrassed Prateek was, his face had turned red and there were beads of sweat on the bridge of his nose.

'I understand, Prateek. Thank you for all your help,' Paul said reassuringly, patting Prateek's arm.

'Sir, I will help you as much as I can. I owe my life to another foreigner like Zoya ma'am. Had she not been kind to me, I would have ended up becoming one of the professional pimps of Sonagachi, or be pressed into sex work.'

Paul decided that he would ask to include Prateek's story in the film as well.

As Paul started his recce, he realized that even with Ganesh accompanying him, filming in Sonagachi was a challenge. Not only was he a white man, the cameras he carried made him too conspicuous. He could feel the hostility all around him.

Some of the women threw their choicest abuse at Ganesh. Paul didn't understand what they were saying but there was no mistaking the tone and the body language.

'What are they saying, Ganesh?' Paul asked.

Ganesh looked embarrassed. 'They have no manners, sir!

They don't know who you are…' Ganesh said.

'But I am nobody and why should they care, in any case.'

'They have no respect for anyone. I cannot repeat what they said,' Ganesh's face was red with embarrassment.

'Okay, okay…I have a pretty good idea. But why do you blame them? We need to understand them by stepping into their shoes, isn't it? Paul said gently.

'Sir, they know me very well and the work that Durjoy is doing to rehabilitate the next generation. But they are so insensitive, even when I'm with a foreign guest,' Ganesh said angrily, leading Paul away to another lane.

'Ganesh, they probably feel that I'm capturing their misery and their helplessness. They are well within their rights to be angry,' Paul said. But he was not one to give up easily.

That evening, Paul shared his concerns with Father Julius. They had finished eating dinner and had moved to the veranda with their coffee cups. Zoya had excused herself and gone to bed. Her long, gruelling days with Durjoy left her exhausted and ready for bed the minute she finished eating dinner.

Ever since Paul and Zoya had moved in to Father Julius's residence, they had started eating a mix of Bengali and continental food. The priest had suggested that this was one way to acclimatize. Both Paul and Zoya loved the hot fluffy rotis and the curries that Jerry, the Odia Christian cook, rustled up for them. Though the food seemed heavy and rather oily and spicy, gradually the taste grew on them and they got used to the local food. They realized that this was the right kind of food for the hot and humid weather of Kolkata. Paul and Zoya found themselves looking forward to trying new dishes at every meal. Zoya took pictures and made copious notes of the ingredients used and the methods of cooking.

'This is really a tough place, this Sonagachi. It will take a long time to break the ice...' Paul said.

'Perhaps you could take the kids with you. That will make your job easier...' Father Julius suggested.

'You're right, Father. That's what Prateek suggested. I had wanted to wait until we had the entire group together, but I could start with the four kids we have so far,' Paul said.

'If you have the kids with you as you move around the locality, you will see the change in attitude among the women immediately. They will automatically associate you with an NGO that is working for the benefit of their children. Naturally, they will become more trusting of you... They won't welcome you with open arms, but perhaps some of the hostility will be blunted. At Sonagachi, women in their prime are so busy that they hardly have time for their kids and it is a great relief to see them safe and cared for by someone else.'

◆

Prateek was worried. He knew that getting Lakshmi to be part of Paul's experiment would not be easy. There were two hurdles that he needed to overcome. First, he would have to broach it with Malati and seek her permission. This was daunting, especially now that she had started Lakshmi's training. The only ray of hope was the fact that she was in dire need of money and Paul had agreed to pay, immediately and regularly. But that would mean a break in Malati's plans for Lakshmi and it would mean allowing her to be away from home for many hours among strangers who were foreigners...

Prateek tossed and turned in his bed at night, unable to sleep, trying to come up with the best argument to convince Malati. He also worried about how Lakshmi would take this. Their last real conversation had been months ago, before Saraju died. They had started out as playmates, best friends and there was once a spark of something more. But their relationship had undergone a big change since he had become more involved in Durjoy. She had often been short and dismissive with him. Lakshmi felt that Prateek was no longer part of her world. If he was being honest with himself, he felt that as well. Since Saraju died, Lakshmi had become rather taciturn. They spoke very infrequently. But he knew what a great chance this could be for her and though it was far-fetched, it just might just help her shake free of Sonagachi. He decided to tackle Malati first, the next morning.

'Malati mashi, how are you? Are you busy? Can I come in?' Prateek climbed up the stairs. Malati was breaking a piece of coal with a hammer in one corner of the veranda. It was a familiar and comforting sight; he had seen Saraju in the same pose so often. Saraju would often send Prateek to fetch water for her. When he came back with the buckets, she would treat him to a batasha or some pickle from one of the plastic jars she kept hidden in the iron trunk underneath her bed.

'Aae, aae, Prateek, how have you been?'

'Good, Mashi. How is everything?'

'As you see. How handsome you look in your jeans and T-shirt! I wouldn't have recognized you had I seen you on the street somewhere.'

'Mashi, now you're joking. Here, I got you some sweets and your favourite paan.'

'Oh, thank you, my boy! How kind of you! May Golapi's soul be blessed!' Malati sounded happy.

She wiped her hands on her sari and accepted the packets eagerly.

'I don't see Lakshmi…where is she?' asked Prateek

'I've just sent her to Suhani. Her training has started,' Malati said carefully. She knew how Prateek felt about her daughter getting into the sex business.

'Mashi, I've come to talk to you about Lakshmi,' Prateek said quickly, not wanting to hear anything more about the training.

Malati put down the sweets and the paan on a kitchen shelf and turned around. Prateek cleared his throat and was about to start when Malati started talking.

'See, Prateek, I don't mind Lakshmi marrying you. In fact, I hoped for the proposal from you. But Lakshmi is all I have and if she goes away with you, who will take care of me? We do not belong to a community where mothers happily give away daughters in marriage, Prateek. So if you marry her and take her away, you will have to promise to pay me a fixed amount every month. You know I'm a plain talker,' Malati said.

'Mashi…' Prateek said quickly before she could go on in this vein. 'I have not come to talk about Lakshmi's marriage…' Prateek looked at Malati, feeling guilty.

'Then what have you come to say?' Malati said impatiently.

'Mashi, I have come to say that there are two foreigners…'

'They want her for the first night? But I have not trained her yet…moreover, they are foreigners…' Malati protested, but she looked eager. Foreigners meant more money.

'Mashi, Mashi…please listen to me. It is not about that at all. I have a plan for her and if you hear me out, you will see that there is monetary benefit involved in it,' Prateek said firmly so that Malati could not interrupt him.

Malati looked at Prateek and waited for him to continue.

'Mashi, these two foreigners are friends of the padre who comes to our NGO. Remember the one who comes here to enrol boys in school?'

'Yes...' Malati was suspicious.

'Now the two foreigners, a man and his wife have come here to work with us. But the man is a film director and wants to make a film on Sonagachi. As part of this film, he wants to form a team of six children whom he will educate for a year and he will film the progress. Lakshmi has a chance to be one of the six children...'

'Prateek, Malati is not a child...she is ready to sit and she has no time to waste on such things!' she said dismissively.

'You call this waste, Mashi? She will learn English, eat and dress well. Don't you want that for her?'

'See, Prateek, I am under too much pressure to make a living. I don't have time for such daydreaming. You choose someone else instead of Lakshmi. Moreover, where is the guarantee that they won't try to take advantage of Lakshmi? After all, they are sahibs with a lot of power and money!'

'Mashi, I am your guarantee for that. They are good people who want to do something good for our women and children here. They will treat Lakshmi like their daughter. Moreover, they are willing to pay for Lakshmi's absence during the day.'

Finally, Prateek was saying something that Malati wanted to hear.

'How much will they pay? For how long will Lakshmi be away? Her absence will mean that I will have to share the load of the housework.'

Prateek felt a small flutter of hope. 'You quote your price,

Mashi. I will try to convince them. I will ask them and find out how many hours Lakshmi needs to be out. And yes, Keka, Basanti didi's daughter will also be part of the team. The other four boys are Raju, Kartick, Paresh and Phatik…'

Eventually, he was able to negotiate the deal between Paul and Malati. He had to make a similar deal with Keka's mother as well. What seemed like a lot of money to Malati was after all, not all that much for the London arm of the NGO and they were able to come to an agreement.

Once that was done, convincing Lakshmi was surprisingly easy. In fact, Malati did the job for him. When Prateek went back to Malati's house a couple of days later, he found Lakshmi at home.

'Lakshmi, make some tea for Prateek. Here, come and sit by me, son,' Malati shifted a little on the mat on which she was sitting and chopping potatoes.

Prateek sat down on the mat beside Malati, a little surprised at this warm welcome. It was quite unlike the blunt Malati. He looked around the room. Nothing had changed since their childhood. He could almost see Saraju sitting on the bed and looking down at him. He knew she would approve of his attempts to help Lakshmi. She had wanted so much for her granddaughter—a happy middle-class life away from the sex trade. She had also had great expectations of Prateek. The room was dark with years of grime and soot. Clothes, towels and sheets were piled on the clothesline. The framed picture of Goddess Lakshmi that Saraju prayed to had faded so much that it was impossible to tell which deity it was. The sindoor on the frame looked fresh though. Prateek's eyes wandered to the corner where Lakshmi sat by the stove as the water hissed in the pot. She wore a faded pink nightie and had draped a yellow dupatta over it. Prateek had seen her pick up the dupatta from the clothesline when he had walked in. She hadn't glanced at Prateek even once, but she looked calm, much to his relief. His eyes followed her hand as it stirred sugar into the tea in the three glasses. She wore glass bangles that made a soothing tinkling sound.

'Prateek, have your sahib-mem agreed to pay me ₹1,500 every month?' Malati wanted to confirm.

Prateek nodded.

'They cannot take her anywhere without telling me and definitely no late nights…' Malati went on with her demands. It was a long list, but nothing that Paul or Zoya could object to, he knew. Prateek knew that he was forcing Lakshmi on Paul, but it was his only hope to get her out. He began dreaming of possibilities for her outside of Sonagachi.

'Your tea has gone cold…shall I heat it up?' Lakshmi broke into Prateek's reverie. He started. Lakshmi was sitting on the mat by him. Malati was no longer in the room.

'Shall I heat up your tea?' Lakshmi repeated, a smile playing on her lips.

'Ah, no, thanks. I'll drink it,' Prateek smiled, a little embarrassed at having been caught lost in thought.

'No problem. Tell me about the project. Ma has left us alone so that we can renew our friendship,' Lakshmi said sweetly.

Prateek was delighted that Lakshmi could see the advantage in this plan.

'Lakshmi, you just have to cooperate with me. I promise, you'll never have to enter the trade and will lead a good life…I will ensure that…you just need to trust me…' Prateek said, his voice full of emotion. He met Lakshmi's gaze squarely. She looked away and nodded, seeming thoughtful but not fully convinced.

◆

The following Monday, Paul came face-to-face with six serious looking children. It was apparent that they were dressed in their best clothes and had been instructed to be on their best behaviour. They all sat on the mat in a line, their powdered faces looking down at the floor.

'Hullo, kids, hullo, young ladies, how do you do?' Paul said, bowing theatrically.

The giggles that they had been holding in escaped. The youngest, Phatik, clapped.

'Delighted to meet all of you,' Paul said, taking the cover off the camera lens and aiming it at the children, who looked surprised but kept smiling all the same.

By the time Prateek came in fifteen minutes later, the children and Paul were no longer being formal with each other. The kids were already happily posing for Paul, who was speaking to them in English, which they obviously did not understand.

'Sir, shall I introduce the team to you?'

'Shall I try first?'

Paul started pointing at the children one after the other. 'Kartick, Raju, Paresh, Lakshmi, Keka and, finally, little Phatick…' Paul scooped the six-year-old up and lifted him onto his shoulders as Phatick squealed with laughter.

Prateek was surprised at how quickly Paul had gotten through to the kids. The two girls were still a little reserved, but the younger kids had become comfortable in no time.

The next few months were a dream for the children. They

would turn up at the Durjoy office at 9.30 a.m. sharp, bathed, dressed and ready for the day. They would be given breakfast there and then wait for Paul and Zoya who would arrive by 10 a.m. The children looked forward to this meal at the start of the day and never missed it. They usually spent half the day on classroom learning and spent the rest of the day taking photographs and videos as they wandered around the city. For the morning session, Zoya got hold of English, Math, Science, Geography and History textbooks that were taught in English-medium schools in the state and tried her best to teach them in batches.

They were quick and intelligent, but they had so much to catch up on. They had all gone to the free Corporation-run school nearby, but had attended irregularly. They knew the English alphabet and how to spell simple words. On some days, it all felt hopeless, but Zoya would not give up easily.

The sessions with Paul and the cameras meant that the group sometimes wandered around Sonagachi and at other times they ventured out to places like Victoria Memorial, the ghats of the Ganga, Indian Museum and the Maidan. On some days they would go to the Singha Palace. The two caretakers knew Paul by now and would admit the party. They stopped warning them about the dangers of climbing to the first floor. Paul and the kids discovered a ladder that the workers used. They used this to climb to the first floor and explore the roof.

Prateek had suggested that they take someone from Durjoy to interpret between the kids and adults. But Paul demurred. 'It is sheer desperation to understand each other that will help us learn the others' language. If they need to learn English, we need to learn Bengali, isn't it?' he had said. And indeed the tactic worked.

Slowly, they had started understanding each other. As the kids improved their English, Paul and Zoya picked up a smattering of Bengali. The kids taught him and Zoya some of their games. Zoya would use the evening sessions to make up games around learning each other's language. Soon all the children were able to speak simple sentences. Zoya had made simple speaking modules for the children and encouraged them to repeat words and sentences with her.

Paul gave each of the kids an inexpensive fixed lens camera, asking them to shoot anything they found interesting. They had fun taking pictures and videos of each other and everything around them. Paul would interview them at times and at other times he would record them singing songs or playing games.

On the days that they decided to spend in Sonagachi, it was a lot easier, now that Paul had the children with him. The denizens of the locality ignored the cameras for the most part and slowly became used to the foreigner in their midst. The group even managed to enter some of the homes and talk to the women when they were free. Sometimes the women standing outside their doors to solicit customers would laugh and joke with the team, some would even solicit Paul, only to be reprimanded by Lakshmi or Keka. But Paul took it in a good-natured way.

The children carried their happy tales back. The happiest among the group were Lakshmi and Keka. They knew that it was probably temporary freedom from the life that awaited them, but they welcomed the respite and did their best to learn and keep Paul and Zoya happy in the hope that their freedom would last a little while longer.

◆

'Bravo! Marvellous! What magic have you guys done with the children?' Father Julius was ecstatic. 'They look smart and speak so well. Look at their smiles and their confidence. Unbelievable!' It was about six months into the project, and Paul finally shared the footage of the kids. Father Julius was surprised.

'The credit goes entirely to Zoya, Father. She has worked very hard with them every day. And I'm so happy that you can see the improvement,' Paul said excitedly.

'Father, they are all very intelligent. They just needed someone to teach them and care about them…' Zoya said quickly.

'No, Zoya, credit where it is due. I know we have miles to go before we reach the goal we've set for ourselves. But we have come so far, thanks to you.'

'Father, you must spend the day with us and see for yourself,' Paul said.

'Why don't we go to Chandernagore on Saturday and spend the entire day there? We're having such a lovely winter and I'm sure all of us will enjoy a small picnic,' Father Julius suggested.

Paul and Zoya agreed enthusiastically.

On the appointed day, the group left with a big picnic basket in a van—the vehicle was owned by the church and was often used for work at St Andrew's School.

'Good morning, Father!' the children shouted happily as he approached the van. The priest was wearing jeans and a T-shirt for a change. He carried his guitar case and a bag that looked full and heavy.

'Good morning, children! Off we go,' he said, taking his seat beside the driver and pulling the door shut.

The children were a little shy at first, but soon Father Julius had them singing songs and making conversation with him.

'Lakshmi, shall we sing a carol?' Zoya asked Lakshmi.

'Sure, ma'am…which one?'

'Our favourite one…' Zoya and Lakshmi exchanged a glance and then Lakshmi started…

'Long time ago in Bethlehem…' her voice was sweet and full of feeling. The rest of the children joined in. Father Julius asked the driver to roll up the windows and switch on the air conditioner so that he could hear them. When they finished, everyone clapped in approval, Father Julius most loudly.

'They're all very good, I want to include them in my church choir, what do you say, Zoya?' Father Julius asked.

Paul and Zoya beamed. Lakshmi and Keka exchanged glances and squeezed each other's hands.

The van traversed the narrow lanes and by-lanes of Chandernagore and, an hour and a half later, finally rolled on to the Strand. The Strand and the massive colonial buildings that line it are the last remnants of the erstwhile French colony that existed there.

The group got off at the Ranir Ghat on the Strand. Then they walked on the raised walkway by the Hooghly. The sky was clear and a weak winter sun made the walk by the wide river particularly pleasurable. Father Julius walked on, lecturing the group about the history of the buildings and of Chandernagore in general. He spoke in a mix of Bengali and English—the children understood most of what he was saying. He also managed to engage the children in conversation and gauge their comprehension and critical thinking ability. The priest led them on to the Durgacharan Rakshit pavilion—a shaded, columned seating arrangement overlooking the Hooghly and embellished with stucco works and floral designs.

'Let me tell you the story of how the British, who ran a successful colony not too far from here, laid their eyes on Chandernagore to rout it,' Father Julius sat them down and continued with his story.

'You mean Kolkata, where the British East India Company was headquartered,' Zoya interjected.

'Correct. Kolkata is less than forty kilometres away. Chandernagore was under French control. The British found the existence of an enemy empire so close by unacceptable. The French governor of Chandernagore, Dupleix, who was an able administrator and extremely popular among the people, lost the fort to the British commanders Robert Clive and Charles Watson in 1756. Chandernagore then went back and forth between the British and French…'

Father Julius knew a lot about the French, Portuguese, Danish and Dutch colonies that dotted the Hooghly at that time.

'I cannot thank you enough for bringing us here, Father. It is like turning the pages of history…' Paul said. He then wandered off to get footage of the surroundings and made plans to come back.

After more light conversation and a big picnic lunch, the group started back. While the children dozed off in their seats, Father Julius made plans with Paul and Zoya.

'Let the children visit us at the church tomorrow morning. I will give each of them a project to do. They will write about the outing in their mother tongue. They will be asked to use as many English expressions as they want. The younger ones will have the choice of expressing themselves through drawings and oral presentations. I will assess their work with the help of a teacher. If they are able to reach the level of proficiency that is required, I will admit the boys in my school while the nuns at the neighbouring Baptist Mission can take the girls. What do you think?' Father Julius asked.

'That will be wonderful!' Zoya exclaimed.

'If we put them in good schools, they will thrive...' Paul added.

Though there was nothing concrete yet, Paul and Zoya felt hopeful. Excitement was building inside them.

◆

Lakshmi and Keka were admitted to Class VII at the Baptist Mission School. They were both too old for the class but did not look out of place because the school admitted children who had dropped out but had been brought within the fold of education once again with the help of NGOs.

While Lakshmi had not cared much for school earlier, now that she had the support of Durjoy, she started enjoying learning. With Paul and Zoya in her life, everything seemed to have changed—the clothes, the food, the hours away from home in clean and happy environs... The new school, complete with the two sets of uniforms, the school bag and books also felt different.

But before this could happen, Malati had to be placated once again. When Prateek went to Malati to explain that Lakshmi would now be away from home from 9 a.m. to 5 p.m. she erupted. Prateek had to make her see how this would help Lakshmi.

'Mashi, why can't you dream of a life outside Sonagachi for Lakshmi? She can look after you even then! She doesn't necessarily have to sit to earn, isn't it?'

'Look, Prateek, what happened with you can never happen to Lakshmi because she is a woman who has to earn her living on her back. If she had any other destiny, you would have married her, isn't it?' Malati threw a challenge at Prateek.

He looked away. 'Look, Mashi, I can only tell you that sometimes dreams do come true, otherwise someone as famous as Paul uncle would not have landed up in Sonagachi and chosen Lakshmi to be one of the members of his team,' he said.

'I don't know them and there is no reason for me to trust them. Yes, they are giving me some money to pay for Lakshmi's absence. So now if they want her to be away for a longer time, they should pay more!' Malati said.

Prateek heard the greed in her voice. He loathed this negotiation, but had no choice.

◆

'Great, Lakshmi! This is such a beautiful letter!' Zoya had just read Lakshmi's letter to her grandmother. It was a Saturday afternoon and Lakshmi and Keka were in Durjoy. They were being taught letter writing in class and Lakshmi had written a letter to her grandmother in heaven, telling her all about her new life.

'Thank you, ma'am. The teacher was happy too. She said that mine was the best letter in class!'

'I can see that. She has put a remark above her signature. Writing to your granny in heaven is a brilliant idea. That's very creative, Lakshmi,' Zoya congratulated her ward. 'But you need to work harder at your Math. You got such a simple sum wrong!'

'Sorry, ma'am. I should have been more careful. But I don't like Math…it's always been like this. I like English, History,

Geography, Bengali…'

'I know that, Lakshmi, but you won't be able to do well in your school leaving exam unless you start liking Math. It is a very crucial subject. I shall ask Shashi to come to teach you thrice a week now,' Zoya said.

Shashi was a private tutor who had been appointed to teach Math to the children. More volunteers had been roped in to help the children with other subjects and all of them were showing remarkable progress. But they had a lot of catching up to do and needed extra lessons and tuitions.

As Lakshmi bent over the notebook, Zoya noticed that she looked especially beautiful in the red skirt and off-white lace top. Her thick hair was done up in a bun that showed off her long neck. The slender, tall and dusky Lakshmi was growing more and more attractive by the day.

Zoya had bought a few sets of clothes for all the children. Lakshmi was wearing one of these sets and it suited her well. Zoya's clothes and shoes also fit Lakshmi, so she would often give the girl some of her clothes and shoes. She gave Keka, who was much shorter and wouldn't fit into her clothes, some of her accessories. Lakshmi treasured her new clothes—she kept them carefully in her trunk. Her grandmother's trunk had now become hers.

'Keka, show me your work,' Zoya turned to the other girl who had been dreamily staring out the window.

Later that evening, Lakshmi was thrilled to be taking home some treats. A group of foreign visitors had come to see Father Julius and brought boxes of pastries, cookies and savoury snacks. He made sure to send a goody bag to Durjoy so that the children could take them home.

'Ma, look what yummy snacks I got today,' Lakshmi announced excitedly as she walked into the house.

Malati had just finished with a client, who paid and left. 'I'm coming,' Malati said, stepping out of the room to go downstairs. She had collected the used condom in a plastic wrapper to dispose of it.

'Ma, I'm making some tea for us,' Lakshmi said happily.

'I'll eat quickly but this was the first customer of the day, Lakshmi. I cannot afford to sit idle for long,' Malati said before going down the stairs.

By the time Malati cleaned up and came back upstairs, Lakshmi had laid out the food and made tea.

'Paltu is no good. He is not able to get me good customers these days. I ended up having a huge row with this middle-aged man whom Paltu brought this afternoon. He said he is a first timer…' Malati complained.

Lakshmi saw how disgusted her mother looked despite all that good food she laid out in front of her. But she kept silent.

'…So I asked him to pay me the money in advance. He said he would pay me more than the agreed sum but only if he was satisfied. I told him straight out that we don't leave things to chance in Sonagachi and asked him to fuck off. He got very angry and called me filthy names. It turned into an ugly fight. Finally Paltu came running and pacified him…harami saala…'

'Ma, please cool down. Paltu would not have brought a troublesome client on purpose. We're not doing all that badly, are we?' Lakshmi asked, pushing the box of food towards her mother.

'Oh yes, you think your sahib is giving me so much money that I can sit on the bed and fan myself to sleep. Don't talk rubbish, Lakshmi, and don't give me your two-bit advice. I know what I'm doing. Stop putting on your artificial manners with me,' Malati said angrily.

She took her pick from the box of goodies, nevertheless, and sipped her tea.

Lakshmi felt a burst of irritation but held her tongue. These days she tried to keep the peace with her mother no matter the provocation. Nothing mattered more to her than going to school and learning from Paul uncle and Zoya aunty. The fact that she and the five other children had been 'adopted' by the sahibs and placed in schools had become the topic of conversation in Sonagachi. Many mothers had started putting in requests to Durjoy to let their kids also be part of this 'new system'. Many of Malati's friends congratulated her, but behind it all was envy. Some even sowed the seeds of doubt in her mind. Why should the sahibs want to teach her daughter English and make a decent girl out of her? Were they planning to adopt her? Malati scrutinized Lakshmi every day. She had indeed changed—she glowed with happiness, looked healthy, clean and certainly out of place in Malati's home these days. But Lakshmi did not neglect her duties at home. While they now had a maid for washing and cleaning, Lakshmi had taken on the entire responsibility of cooking in the evening. There was a distinct change in her behaviour towards her mother; she was polite and respectful, so despite Malati's suspicions, their relationship improved somewhat.

9.

Lakshmi had been waiting impatiently by the tea stall for over fifteen minutes when Keka came hurrying up the street.

'Keka, why are you so late? I was about to walk on alone!' Lakshmi scolded Keka.

Lakshmi and Keka walked together to Durjoy every morning and took the hand-pulled rickshaw to school from there. The same rickshaw dropped them at Durjoy every evening where they had their evening classes.

Keka's eyes were red, it was obvious that she had been crying and she avoided looking at Lakshmi. They hurried to the rickshaw. Once they started moving towards the school, Lakshmi asked Keka again.

'What's wrong?'

'Lakshmi di, Ma is not well. So I had to help her with the housework…and then…' Keka stopped.

'What happened? Tell me!'

'Ma is not well and so couldn't work…that man who came for her…tried to…'

'Tried to… Did he force himself on you?'

'Yes. He pulled me towards himself, I turned around and slapped him. He tried to put his hands under my dress, I screamed and bit him. But my mother…she got up from the bed and banged my head against the wall…' Keka started weeping.

Lakshmi put an arm around her and tried to console her. This made her cry harder and she broke down.

Keka continued, sniffling, 'Didi…I will run away from here. I will run away with Ajoy…' she sounded desperate.

'Don't you dare!' growled Lakshmi. 'Do you know what will happen if you do that?'

'I know, Didi, they will blame Prateek da and uncle and aunty…'

'Yes, they will. They are trying their best to help us. Remind your mother that she is being paid for your time, there's no need to make you take on her clients.'

'I know, Didi, but my mother feels Malati mashi is getting more than her. She keeps saying she wants to talk to Zoya aunty about this.'

Lakshmi didn't know what to say. This was an uncomfortable topic. Her mother was being paid more and this had led to heated arguments between Malati and Basanti mashi. Lakshmi spoke to Zoya and Prateek about this. Prateek had impressed on both Malati and Lakshmi to keep the amount they were being paid to themselves. Lakshmi swore that she hadn't said anything. In any case, he had suspected that Malati had been bragging about the money. He decided to speak to Paul, but he was rather embarrassed about it. What would the kind foreigner think of these greedy women? Did they have no self-respect?

Prateek managed to get Keka's mother a little more money. But he warned her not to expect any more because Paul and Zoya were upset and might decide to drop Keka from the programme if she nagged them anymore. The crisis was averted and it looked like things might go back to normal. Until Keka made a huge mistake.

One day after school, Lakshmi was waiting at the gate for Keka. Normally they would meet within ten minutes of school getting over. Lakshmi was usually the first to come out and she would wait for Keka. After having sat there for half an hour, Lakshmi went inside to look for her friend. She was getting annoyed. Keka had made this a habit of late—and they were getting late for classes at Durjoy. She had a good mind to give her a scolding. She checked the classroom, the staff room, the library, the small play area, the toilet and even the seats where they ate their tiffin. Keka was nowhere. Lakshmi's heart sank. She ran downstairs to the gate to ask the rickshaw puller to wait. Then she ran to the principal's office where the nuns had gathered for tea and snacks. The school was empty and the sound of her footsteps seemed to echo her drumming heart.

'Come in, child, what happened?' Sister Margaret, the principal, asked kindly.

'Sister, Keka is missing, I can't find her!' Lakshmi panted, standing at the entrance of the office.

Sister Margaret looked serious. 'Sister Benita! Please ask Meena and the other sweepers to comb the school. Lakshmi, I believe Keka is a neighbour and you know her mother?'

Lakshmi nodded.

'Can you go back with the school guard to check if she has gone home on her own today? You will have to come back and report to me. Can you do that?'

'Sister, our rickshaw is waiting for us, I can take that. It will be faster.'

'Go, child, get me good news,' Sister Margaret said to her,

making the sign of the cross.

Lakshmi got in the rickshaw and first went to Durjoy. She feared that this matter was not going to be resolved easily. Lakshmi rushed into Prateek's cubicle, out of breath. Prateek looked up, surprised. When she told Prateek that she wasn't able to find Keka, he was shocked. They sped to Keka's house. She wasn't there. But her mother was and she immediately knew something was terribly wrong. She started cursing Prateek and wailing loudly that her daughter was lost and that she might be dead. In no time a crowd gathered. Some people consoled Basanti, saying the girl would be found, she couldn't have gone far. Others vented about Durjoy and the foreigners it was bringing into their lives.

Prateek saw that the situation was getting dangerous. He assured Basanti he would do all that he could and, extricating Lakshmi from the crowd, went back to Durjoy. He told Paul and Zoya what had happened. Sister Margaret had in the meantime informed Father Julius, who got to Durjoy in no time.

Zoya was pale and shaken. 'Should we go to Basanti first?' she asked.

'Ma'am, it's not safe for you to even stay here. There is a crowd at Basanti mashi's house and they are trying to fan hatred for the NGO and for you and sir. Let us leave Sonagachi immediately and head for the school,' Prateek suggested. He knew Keka's mother would forget all the gratitude she had expressed earlier in a split second. She and her neighbours and friends would create a huge row and place the blame squarely on the NGO. This was how things worked here. No one was a permanent friend, you could take nothing for granted. A small misunderstanding could bring everything down.

'Should I go back home?' Lakshmi asked in a small voice.

'No, you come with us, Lakshmi. Keka's mother will start grilling you, thinking that you might have had a hand in this,' Father Julius said.

Paul and Father Julius had encouraged Sister Margaret to call the police once they were sure that Keka was nowhere in school.

'Keka is so docile and obedient. She could not have left the school on her own. Do you think someone has convinced her to leave?' Zoya wondered aloud.

Lakshmi's throat tightened. She had to tell Zoya something, but couldn't bring herself to.

As they left in the van, Zoya gathered herself and started asking Lakshmi what else she knew.

Lakshmi broke down. She had been keeping Keka's secret for a long time and blamed herself.

From the moment she realized Keka was missing, Lakshmi suspected that Keka had finally run away with Ajoy. The young man would often wait around outside school. Lakshmi had admonished Keka about this. Keka told her that they were in love and hoped to marry. But they were worried about what her mother would say. Ajoy gave Keka some money every now and then and brought her little gifts. Keka was thrilled and believed it was a sign that he really cared for her. But Lakshmi distrusted him. He had shifty eyes and always sped off when he saw Lakshmi coming out.

'Why does he come to school to meet you? If the teachers find out, you'll be in trouble!' Lakshmi had said to Keka.

'Ma doesn't like him. So we can't meet at home, Didi. Where else can we see each other?'

'I don't think you should trust him, Keka. Think what an opportunity we're getting at school. Study and try and get out of here. This boy will only land you in trouble.'

'Didi, please don't say anything to Zoya aunty or Prateek da.'

'I don't feel comfortable about the whole thing. I will get a bad name because of you,' Lakshmi had said, not bothering to hide her irritation.

But Keka had begged her and she had kept the secret.

Prateek was mad at her. He looked dark with anger and Lakshmi cowered. 'How irresponsible of you!' he shouted.

Paul and Father Julius tried to calm him down.

'She knew that it was dangerous for Keka to meet this boy. Lakshmi should have reported it to us for her own safety and ours!' Prateek bellowed from the front seat of the van.

Lakshmi cried even harder.

The police and the people of the neighbourhood launched a search for Ajoy. Keka was found a few days later at a hotel near Sealdah. Ajoy had promised her marriage and then sold her off to a gang that was involved in the flesh trade.

Keka and the other girls who had been found at the hotel were recovered by the police and sent to the state-run home for rescued girls. Zoya had wanted to go and see her immediately, but the rules were very strict and they needed permission to meet her.

Ten days later, Father Julius got permission from the police for Paul and Zoya to visit Sarada Juvenile Home. They could see Keka for half an hour. Zoya packed some clothes and books to leave with Keka. Prateek drove them there. It took them over an hour and a half to reach the home in Baruipur, after fighting endless traffic snarls.

The two-storey building that was the juvenile home was damp and dilapidated. The walls had cracks and the whole placed looked likely to collapse at any minute. There was a dank smell and Zoya shuddered to think of Keka living here. At Sonagachi, her living conditions had not been any better until she became part of Paul's project. And, in any case, she lived with her mother, it was her home. Here, she was almost in prison. How could this hellhole be a home for children to rehabilitate them? Zoya wondered.

The guard at the door took them into the office where a gaunt, severe looking woman dozed on a wooden chair. A thick register was on the table in front of her. She wore a faded nightie with a dupatta draped around her shoulders. The room was dark and damp, a small bulb glowed weakly and an old ceiling fan creaked overhead.

'Didi, they have come…' the guard said.

'Umm..?'

'The visitors for the new girl, they are here.'

The woman roused herself and looked at them closely. 'Okay. Come in all of you. Sit down,' she indicated the bench beside her. Paul, Zoya and Prateek walked in.

'I was told by the police that only two foreigners would be coming to see that girl, Keka. But why have you come?' the woman asked Prateek. 'I do not like indiscipline. This home is a secure place where visitors come only with police permission. No one can just walk in here. You have to leave now,' she ordered Prateek.

Paul and Zoya looked at her helplessly.

'Didi, I have come as an interpreter. They cannot speak or understand Bengali. Our padre spoke to the police about this while seeking permission,' Prateek explained.

'Okay, okay. Rupa! Rupa! Come here fast…' she called out

loudly from her perch. A thin worn-out looking young woman peered into the room.

'Go and get that new girl here at once,' ordered the woman.

'Okay, Chuni didi. That girl who came with the group of five? She had other women with her who were taken to Kamala Home? Isn't that the case, Didi?' the woman called Rupa asked.

'Have I asked you to tell me a story? Go and bring that girl! Quick!'

In about ten minutes, Keka walked into the room, looking scared. Zoya started to walk towards Keka.

'No, no, no, no...that is not allowed. Please stay back!' the woman hollered in Bengali, gesturing at Prateek to tell his friends to stay in place.

'Ma'am, she is asking you to stay away from Keka.'

Keka sat down on the metal chair meant for inmates, facing Paul and Zoya, her head hanging low.

'How are you, Keka?' Zoya said softly.

'I am fine, ma'am, how are you?' she replied so softly that she was barely audible.

'We are not good without you, Keka.'

'I am so sorry, ma'am. I shouldn't have done this to you,' Keka said as tears rolled down her cheeks.

'You shouldn't have done this to yourself, my girl. You had so much potential. But let's see what we can do now. We can start figuring out how to get you released from here.'

Chuni was listening to them intently, trying to read their expressions. She was quite surprised that Keka was speaking to the foreign lady in English. The word 'release' caught her attention.

'No, no, no English here. Tell those sahibs that they cannot use code language here. It is not allowed for the safety of the girls,' Chuni said.

'Didi, don't worry. She is like a mother to her. She is not trying to break any of your rules,' Prateek said. He then started chatting with the woman so that she was distracted until Zoya and Paul finished.

'No, ma'am. I'm okay here. I have a bed, they feed me. It feels like a jail, but I am safe.'

'Don't you want to come back to us?'

'No, ma'am. You will not stay here permanently to look after me. My mother is so angry with me. She said that I have ruined my life and hers. I know she will force me to start sex work once I go back. I don't want that.'

◆

'We lost her, Paul. An innocent life wasted,' Zoya wept on the way back.

Paul sighed and swallowed the lump in his throat.

After Keka's misfortune, everyone at Durjoy had been worried that Malati would use it as an excuse to pull Lakshmi out of the programme. Surprisingly, Malati didn't make too much of a fuss. She had had arguments with Basanti about the money and now she felt perversely vindicated. Besides, she told Lakshmi, Keka had brought this misfortune on herself.

So when Zoya went to talk to her, she did not threaten to stop Lakshmi's education. 'Keka's is just another story, memsahib. This is not new around here. But, memsahib, it will soon be time for Lakshmi to start working. I plan to introduce her during the pujas next year. I hope you will be through with her by then,' Malati said.

'We are a year into the project. We have another year to go. Let Lakshmi finish her school, then maybe we can get her a scholarship—'

Malati interrupted. 'Already Lakshmi thinks she has become too good for Sonagachi and the work that we do here. She keeps throwing her English at me and even talks back. You better explain to her that at the end of all this she has to return here and work the way other girls do.'

◆

Lakshmi missed Keka but realized she had to put it behind her. She had become a lot more serious. No doubt her mother's refrain that this life was not going to continue was on her mind.

'Ma'am, what will happen to me when you go away?' Lakshmi asked Zoya.

They had gone to the Botanic Gardens at Howrah. It was a Sunday. Paul had read about the four-hundred-year-old banyan tree there and wanted to see it. They had brought a picnic and had opened it up on the rolling green fields surrounding the banyan tree.

While Paul went about with his camera, Zoya and Lakshmi sat on the mat, chatting. The four boys explored, running around and yelling to each other.

'We won't just abandon you, you know that, Lakshmi,' Zoya replied.

'Ma'am, my mother reminds me of my inevitable future every day. I switch off when I leave the house, but have to go back to that reality again in the evening,' Lakshmi said. She had wanted to bring this up with Zoya for some time now.

'Have faith, Lakshmi. Do your best in school and learn. That is all we can do.'

'I don't want to get into the profession, but who will feed me and my mother if I don't? Sometimes I think I should run away from home. I can work as a maid somewhere...'

'Take that silly thought out of your head, Lakshmi. You saw what happened to Keka, do you want to end up in a home like that?'

'All this,' Lakshmi said, taking in her surroundings, 'seems like a dream. This beautiful garden, the trees, the food, the fun that we have, even the studies...but how long can dreams last?' Lakshmi said.

Zoya's heart went out to the talented girl. There was nothing of the shy young girl that Zoya had met a little over a year ago. Lakshmi had turned into a beautiful, smart and well-behaved teenager. She felt gratified that her efforts had paid off but unsure and deeply worried about how they could continue to support Lakshmi and the others. Zoya knew that Lakshmi was asking her to take her away from Sonagachi. But only a miracle could make that possible.

A few days later, Zoya brought her worries to Paul and Father Julius.

'Father, can we chalk out a more concrete plan for the kids? What will happen to them after Paul completes his film in about a year?' Zoya asked.

'Yes, Father, the year will go by before we realize it. We have to see how we can keep these kids on the path they've started on,' Paul said. This was something he had been worrying about as well. Both Paul and Zoya had become attached to the kids and were concerned about their well-being.

'I've been looking at our options as well. We could try for a local adoption. This would mean that the children would continue to live with their mothers, but their education and other needs will be funded by the adoptive parents. We could approach a local corporate house to help with this. Durjoy can be the mediating NGO.'

'That would be a wonderful option,' Zoya agreed.

'The other option would be to ask Hope for Life to continue to fund them, which they would do if the kids show promise in their studies.'

'Father, you know how they have progressed. They have not failed in any subject so far, and it's only been a year.'

'I agree. The boys will sail through school if we are able to arrange for their expenses.' He paused, looking pained. 'But the one you pin your hopes on, Lakshmi, will not be able to complete her education unless a miracle happens. All this education and exposure is only making her mother firmer in her resolve. She thinks Lakshmi will now be worth a lot more,' Father Julius said.

Zoya looked away. They all knew this was the reality.

'Please let's try our best for her…whatever it takes,' Zoya said softly.

'I am sorry to say this, Paul, Zoya, but I hope you understand that Lakshmi's mother only lets her continue here because you're paying her. To her, this is an exchange, pure and simple. The boys' mothers can be convinced that education will give them a good job and that they will earn well and help support them. But the girls in Sonagachi, their lives are cast in stone,' Father Julius said.

A pall of gloom descended on the room. They were all silent for a while. As if by agreement, they looked at the painting on the wall. It was a painting of Mother Mary and Baby Jesus done in watercolours with a distinctly Indian aesthetic. It was one of Lakshmi's paintings that Zoya and Paul had fallen in love with. Lakshmi told them that she had pictured her grandmother and herself while painting it.

'Can we arrange for their adoption in the UK?' Paul asked.

'Getting the mothers to agree will be almost impossible. Again, the boys' mothers, maybe. But if they ask to be compensated, will you be able to arrange for that kind of money?' Father Julius asked.

'We can try. I know this is going to be tough, Father. Perhaps I am reacting emotionally. When I started this project I had no idea I would get so involved in their lives…' Paul answered.

'A lot also depends on how your film turns out. It could be the vehicle to get the funding you need for these children. Come, come, have faith in God. He cannot let such honest intentions down,' Father Julius said, in an effort to raise flagging spirits.

Zoya decided to broach the subject of adoption with Lakshmi. She wanted to find out what the young girl wanted. Summer holidays would start in a week and term results were expected. Good results meant better chance for adoptions or scholarship funding for all the children.

'I'm sure you'll get top marks in all your subjects this year, even Math,' Zoya joked.

'Thank you, ma'am. It's all thanks to you,' Lakshmi said.

'Lakshmi, if we could manage to get you to come and live with us in the UK while you completed your studies, would you want to?'

Lakshmi stared wide-eyed at Zoya, unable to believe that this was a possibility. 'Oh, my God! Yes, ma'am!' Lakshmi shouted. But then reality caught up with her and she looked deflated. 'But my mother…'

'We'll come and talk to her, what do you say?'

But they had underestimated Malati and mistaken her recent calm for a change of heart. The meeting between Prateek, Paul, Zoya and Malati went badly. She cursed and spat at them and threw them out of the house. They left, sadly, worried that Lakshmi would bear the brunt of it.

For the next few days, there was no news from Lakshmi. There was no school, but she didn't turn up for her classes at Durjoy either. Phatick told Zoya that he had seen Lakshmi with a swollen face, split lip and blood-red eyes. It was clear that her mother had beaten her up.

Malati put Lakshmi under house arrest. She decided to arrange for Lakshmi's first night as soon as she could. But Lakshmi was not a pliant child any longer. She refused to cooperate. She wouldn't eat—she was scared of being drugged and taken for the first night whether she wanted to or not. She threatened to commit suicide. Lakshmi even threatened to go to the local police station and complain against her mother. Prateek came a few times, and explained to Malati that the foreigners were not trying to steal her daughter away.

'You think I'm a fool? She's good-looking and they'll sell her. Fine, let them take her, but if you don't want trouble from me, get them to pay me. What is she worth to them? Ten lakh rupees?' she challenged.

But with Lakshmi proving intractable, she had to relent temporarily—after all, some money would continue to trickle in. Lakshmi was welcomed back at Durjoy but they all felt a sense of frustration. Lakshmi had lost her gaiety and confidence. She was on edge, waiting for the axe to fall.

They continued the routine the next academic year, but Zoya,

Lakshmi, Paul, even Father Julius felt like they were coming to the end of something.

The year flew by. Paul had become welcome in the lanes of Sonagachi, not just in the homes of his students, but through them in the homes of their neighbours. He had made a couple of trips to the UK and had raised funds for filming, even taking on a part-time research assistant from Durjoy and a translator. He was not only documenting the sex workers but also the lives of the children in the Durjoy programme and their amazing and continuous progress. He spoke to educators across the country, filmed in schools that were in low-income areas and travelled to other red-light districts in India.

He found out about the women's customers. Some of them were lonely men whose only sexual outlet was in these lanes. Some of them had perversions that they could not fulfil in their own homes. He also found out about illnesses and sexually transmitted diseases that threatened the women's lives and livelihoods.

But, most of all, he came to know these women as people who were making the best of their situation like everyone else. They were thoroughly professional in their approach. As far as they were concerned, they were doing a job to earn money. And like other people sold goods or services, they were selling their bodies. There was nothing wrong in that. They cared nothing for the world that thought of them as criminals or morally corrupt.

Paul had completed shooting his documentary. He was going to take all his material and use his usual studio in the UK to edit the film before sending it to the British Academy Awards and Cannes Film Festival.

Like Paul had anticipated, the year raced by and soon it was time for Paul and Zoya to leave. They had put their other life on hold, but now they had to go back to that reality. They gave money to the mothers of the four boys, making them promise at the Durjoy office that they would allow their kids to continue with their studies. They met Malati separately and gave her ten thousand rupees. Zoya held Malati's hands and begged her to give them six months.

'We will try our best to get you your quoted price,' Zoya said.

Malati looked away without answering.

Zoya had no idea how they could come up with the money Malati had demanded. Malati had refused to discuss it any further and was being very stubborn, refusing to negotiate. Although she said time and again that all she cared about was money, perhaps letting her daughter go was not all that easy. She was her only family and, surly as Malati was, Lakshmi was all she had. Zoya wondered whether Malati would let Lakshmi go even if they got the money that she demanded.

Lakshmi had had the time to get used to the idea that they would leave, but when the time came, she felt like her heart was broken.

'This is not goodbye forever,' Zoya told her. 'We'll come back and try our best to make sure you can continue studying.'

Lakshmi nodded through her tears—she clung to that hope.

10.

'Lakshmi, great news! Paul uncle's film has won some big award,' Prateek had run all the way from the NGO to Lakshmi's house. He stood there laughing and out of breath.

Lakshmi had been cleaning the kitchen after making the afternoon meal. She stood up, wiping her hands on a towel. 'Really? How did you know?' Lakshmi asked in happy disbelief. Malati also came out of her room.

'Paul uncle called Father Julius and asked him to tell me. Father Julius told the boys in school today!' Prateek said.

'What's next? Is there going to be an award ceremony?' Lakshmi asked.

'It will be on the TV news soon. But uncle and aunty have promised to call today. They told us to watch the BBC news at 2.30 p.m. Mashi, you both must come and watch it at Durjoy,' Prateek said.

Lakshmi's eyes misted over. She wondered if this award might change things. Will they get enough money so that she could go to the UK to study? She looked over and noticed that even Malati was looking pleased at the news.

'So you'll be famous now. That sahib and memsahib should pay you for making their film big,' Malati said.

Lakshmi threw her mother a scornful look.

By the time Lakshmi and Malati reached Durjoy, the boys from the group and their families had placed themselves on the mat in front of the television. After the political and world news, the anchor announced the results of the film awards.

'*The Sex Citadel* is the first film about India to win a BAFTA. A documentary shot in Sonagachi with children of sex workers, the film has won the Critics' Award for Best Film.' On hearing the name of the film, the children and Durjoy staff cheered loudly. A short clip of the film was shown and the children saw themselves on screen. They were ecstatic. The boys would be heroes at school tomorrow. Lakshmi was thrilled but also thoughtful—she was more concerned about how this would help her future. Her mind felt fuzzy and she felt like she was watching things from a great distance. Prateek came forward and gave her a warm hug. She looked up at him for a moment and then looked away.

Father Julius arrived with snacks and soft drinks and soon everyone gave themselves up to the celebration. Paul and Zoya called and spoke to each child individually. They spoke to the mothers as well. The award would be given away at the prestigious Royal Opera House in London. Zoya and Paul had managed to raise funds not only for the travel and accommodation of the children who participated in the film, but also some money that would fund their education.

Since Malati had reacted so badly the last time there had been talk of taking Lakshmi to the UK, Zoya stepped very gingerly. She explained that all the kids would be taken to London and brought back. Zoya knew that Malati would not be easily convinced; she spoke to her for a long while. Malati was overwhelmed by the reaction around her. And perhaps what she saw on screen had made an impact on her. She was polite to Zoya.

'Don't worry, Malati, I will send your daughter back after the award ceremony. This is such an incredible opportunity for your girl, and she will love being here. Please, think about it,' Zoya explained in her broken Bengali over the phone.

'Achha dekhi…' Malati was non-committal.

Paul and Zoya came to Kolkata a month before the event—they were going to accompany the children to the ceremony. More importantly, they had to make arrangements for the future of these children. They had started the process for the passports with the mothers' cooperation. Malati had agreed to do the paperwork, but was standing firm on the money.

In the meantime, the local press had found the story and was taken in by it. The kids, the NGO, Paul and Zoya, even the mothers were interviewed by the many newspaper and TV journalists who thronged Sonagachi. Lakshmi, as the oldest and most articulate, was interviewed by herself. She even took some of the journalists around, talking about her experience and what she had learnt. It was a heady, dreamy time for all of them. The coverage kept going for weeks and Lakshmi had more than her share of fame. She was a well-spoken, lovely looking young girl—the cameras loved her. Sonagachi and the plight of the women and children even became a part of a manifesto of one of the candidates in the local election. But after the news cycle was done with the story, the hubbub died down…and Sonagachi was forgotten once again.

Since the film had been made on Paul's fellowship that was funded by a conglomerate, there was some money that they could use for the children. 'We will divide the money equally among the children's mothers and us. We have also spoken to Hope for Life in the UK and they are willing to partly fund the kids' education there. We will start counselling their parents,' Paul told Father Julius. They had not forgotten Keka. The couple hoped that they could help her start a new life with the money that was rightfully hers. Instead of handing over the money to her mother, they put it in an account in Father Julius's name.

'She won't be in the home for much longer,' said Father Julius. 'Sister Margaret has been keeping in touch with her. When she heard about the award and the prize money, Keka asked if she could open a tailoring shop. We'll get her vocational training and help her set up a shop,' Father Julius promised. 'Prateek has agreed to help with this.'

'We leave her to you, Father, I know you will take care of her,' Paul said. They were relieved that Keka would be able to make a life for herself doing what she wanted. Zoya visited Malati and gave her a cheque for fifty thousand rupees. Malati was overcome by the amount of money and didn't pay attention to what Zoya was saying. Then she realized that Zoya was asking for permission to take her daughter for the award ceremony.

'Ma'am, you have been very kind to Lakshmi. I cannot deny that. But I will need much more than what you've given me to secure my future if Lakshmi is not going to earn.'

'I have given you a cheque for fifty thousand rupees, Malati. Why do you want to destroy your daughter's life? Let her finish studying so that she can earn at a respectable job. Don't you want to give your daughter the best in life?' Zoya entreated.

'Memsahib, you are seeing us from a distance. No matter how many days you spend with us here, you will never understand our life, our reality. No one has been able to get out from this life and earn elsewhere. And those of us who work here have a very short earning period. Most of us are forced into retirement by the time we are forty-five years old. Some of us get beaten up, or the diseases get us. Then there are criminals and the police to deal with...money *is* the single most important factor of our lives,' Malati explained. 'You want to take her with you? Take her, by all means. I will sign whatever paper you want saying that I have willingly given my daughter away for adoption, but not before I get the money.'

'We are ordinary people, Malati. The fact that we are foreigners doesn't mean that we're rich. We've distributed the prize money among the children, keeping just one part for us.' Zoya saw that Malati was not going to relent. 'I will try to arrange for some money and send it with Lakshmi when she returns from the ceremony. Please accept that and allow us time to arrange for Lakshmi's adoption after.'

'I don't want to bargain with you, memsahib. I will consider it my greatest fortune if you take her and keep her with you. I gave birth to her, but I could do nothing to make her happy. I can see how she has started shining under your care. But I would be a fool to just let her go on your word...'

Both women sat in silence for some time and then Zoya got up to leave. It was clear that there was no changing Malati's mind. Paul and Zoya had not been working at their usual jobs for nearly two years. This had drained their savings and they didn't see any way to raise the amount of money that Malati demanded.

Finally it was time for the group to leave for the award ceremony. Lakshmi sobbed when she went to say goodbye at Durjoy. Zoya hugged her tight but didn't make any promises this time. Lakshmi cried as she walked home slowly.

For a while Lakshmi lived in a world of contradictions. Her

neighbours and friends treated her like a celebrity, but there were others who were jealous of her stardom and let her know it. She continued going to school but her heart was no longer in it. What was the point? she wondered. How will knowing algebra help me when I'm pleasuring some disgusting old man?

Malati kept waiting for a call from Zoya or Father Julius about the adoption. Zoya called and spoke to Lakshmi at the Durjoy office but only to find out about how she was doing in school. She did not talk about the adoption. Malati's patience ran out. Prateek confirmed to her that Paul and Zoya had not been able to get the money that she had demanded. He implored her once again to let Lakshmi study, but she refused to talk to him about this anymore. Malati had made up her mind; there was no more reprieve.

Soon Lakshmi went back to Suhani to restart her training. Suhani was a happy woman who loved to laugh and joke. She was also very good at the art of seduction. She had been a very successful sex worker in her time. She taught Lakshmi how to dress so her assets were highlighted, how to do her make-up so that her best features sparkled, the different kisses and sex positions and what men expected and how to pleasure them. She also taught her how to find out what sort of man she was dealing with. Was he someone who wanted conversation and laughter? Did he want a woman to press his feet and massage his back? Did he want sweet approval? Or would he be quick to take offence at false praise? Was he a drunk, abusive? Seeing the truth of a man could not only mean the difference between success and failure. On the fragile streets of Sonagachi, it could mean life or death.

But, first, she had to learn to drink. Suhani handed Lakshmi a small glass of rum. Lakshmi screwed up her nose at the acrid smell. After her first sip, she heaved, sure that she would throw it all up.

Suhani laughed. 'Being drunk is the only way you'll get through the first time. Come on, drink up.'

Lakshmi shuddered. The bitter burning taste of the rum made her retch. She could feel her dreams swirling away into nothingness.

◆

The room had been cleaned and whitewashed with lime for Lakshmi's first night. There were new sheets on the bed and the mattress had been repaired to make it reasonably comfortable. Malati had arranged for Lakshmi to use Paltu's quarters. This way, Malati could continue to use her room. There wasn't enough space for both of them in this house. Malati appeared nonchalant and pragmatic as always, but deep down, she was uncomfortable. Perhaps she didn't want to have to see her daughter with her customers.

Malati had spent money on the repair and furnishing of her daughter's new quarters from the money that Zoya had given her. She also used the money to pay Suhani's dues. Lakshmi had to pay three hundred rupees to her mother as rent, a portion of which would go to Paltu. She would also have to hand over half her daily earnings to her mother in return for food.

It was an age-old Sonagachi custom—'fresh' girls were introduced on Friday or Saturday nights, when the demand soared and the money flowed. She is presented as a fresh offering by her owner. The owner starts an auction for the first night, driving the price as high as possible. And Lakshmi's new-found fame only helped with this. Malati rejected the offers that came from the dhaba owner, the local chemist, the taxi-fleet owner, a clerk who worked in a college and a few others. By this time, the price had become high enough that Malati was happy. Finally, when the owner of a biscuit factory turned up with an offer of seven thousand rupees, Malati agreed. The man, a regular at some of the more expensive brothels at Sonagachi, had a taste for virgins. He had seen Lakshmi on the news and was infatuated. He also belonged to a rich family, the pimp had told her. Most of the money from the first night would go to Malati as was the custom. She would pay the pimp a commission. It was the fee that a new girl pays to her owner for setting her up.

'One day you will thank me for this,' Malati said to Lakshmi as she handed her a cup of tea on that morning. 'It is your association with those sahibs that has spoilt you. But it's time to come back to reality. You're lucky that you have a secure home and a mother as your guardian. You'll never know how difficult life can be here under a mashi.' Although she was speaking in her usual casual tone, there was a knot in her stomach.

Later that afternoon, Suhani came to take Lakshmi to start the preparation. 'Ma, ashchi,' Lakshmi said before leaving for her new quarters. It was the customary goodbye that she said every time she left home, but today it sounded strange to her ears. Her mother didn't respond, didn't turn around from the kitchen stove. Paltu gave her a sympathetic look from the veranda. She felt her eyes smart, but she squeezed them shut and went with Suhani. When they reached her room, Lakshmi saw that some of the elders of Sonagachi and Suhani's girls were waiting for her. It was a special day and Sonagachi elders treated first nights almost like weddings. Lakshmi was bathed and shampooed by the girls.

Then they dried and perfumed her hair with the smoke of incense sticks. They dabbed perfume under her arms, on her neck and between her legs. Every now and then, someone handed her a small glass of rum that she swallowed with a grimace.

'Lie down,' said Suhani, pushing Lakshmi down on the bed. Suhani then pried Lakshmi's knees apart and applied a cold, sticky liquid between her legs. As her hands reached Lakshmi's innermost parts, it burned. Lakshmi squirmed and tried to push Suhani away.

'Ooh! It's burning! Stop!' Lakshmi protested.

'Stop that, the burning will go away. Listen to me now. Let your vaginal muscles relax and then contract so that the gel goes deep inside and works on the vaginal wall. You won't feel the pain when he pushes inside you,' Suhani said. Lakshmi felt the numbness spreading and stopped squirming.

Her hair was done up in a bun and had flowers threaded all around it. Malati had bought a new silk sari for Lakshmi. The girls helped her wear the heavy red sari with gold zari. It played off her dusky skin. Her small earrings and bangles caught the light and threw it back in hundreds of slivers. Lakshmi had become very quiet; her head swam but her heart hammered hard against her chest. All the stories she had heard over the years began to play on her mind. And through it all, she thought of the award function she had missed and her brief, happy days with Zoya aunty and Paul uncle.

Finally it was time. The man who came into her room that night was middle-aged, obese and had a thin sheen of sweat on his forehead. Though Lakshmi was intoxicated, her instincts kicked in and she forgot her training. As soon as he started towards her, she lunged towards the door. The man wasn't expecting this. Lakshmi tried to open the door, but it had been locked from the outside. Girls often lost their nerve on the first night and the women made sure that they locked the door to stop them from running away. The man pulled her roughly back and pushed her onto the bed. 'You thought you could escape?' he asked.

'Uncle, please let me go. I will massage your back, press your tired legs and hands, but please let me go...' Lakshmi managed to stutter.

'Don't worry, my darling. I will be gentle with you. Let's make this as pleasurable as possible for both of us,' the man said, undressing quickly. A scared squeak escaped her as he came towards her and started pulling off her sari. She continued to struggle, and the man became angry.

'Don't fight me, girl. I've paid your greedy mother more than I have ever paid before,' he growled. He ripped off her sari and her blouse. She felt his rough hands on her. He got on top, crushing her under his weight. After this, the night was a blur to Lakshmi. When he finally entered her, she felt an excruciating pain. She screamed. He put a heavy hand over her mouth and started thrusting. That gel didn't work, she thought to herself. When he finished, he slowly climbed off and lay still for a while. Soon, he started snoring. Lakshmi lay frozen on the bed for a while. Then she slowly sat up. Every part of her was hurting and there was a smear of blood on the sheet—proof that the man had deflowered a virgin. Collecting her clothes about her, Lakshmi went to the door and knocked softly. When no one answered, she pulled it open. It had been unlocked at some point. She limped to the bathroom, sat on her haunches and started pouring water over her head from the big tin drum that stood filled to the brim.

The water seemed to soothe away the burning and the pain and washed away her tears.

The next morning, the man stepped out of the room to find Lakshmi sitting quietly outside. 'Did I hurt you too much?' he asked kindly. He didn't seem like the same man who had raped her the previous night. Lakshmi stared at him in surprise, not able to come up with an answer.

'Such is life here, girl. Get used to it. With your looks and class, you will easily get a babu. If he is rich, he will keep you well. So get yourself a wealthy babu. You can make a good future for yourself. Don't be emotional and foolish like these illiterate women. Use your assets to your advantage,' he said shoving a few notes into her hands. 'I've already paid your mother. Keep this for yourself,' he said and left.

◆

Lakshmi quickly became very sought after. She had regular customers and was kept busy getting used to her new life. But something that the biscuit factory owner had said to her kept ringing in her ears. He had been a brute but he highlighted something that Lakshmi had noticed. She was literate, sophisticated and had the ability to move with a higher class of people. She should cash in on this. She came up with a plan. Maybe Keka could help her.

Father Julius had kept his word. He had not only helped Keka out of the juvenile home but had also set up a shop for her. The shop would remain in the name of the parish until she came of age. Once out of the juvenile home, Keka had been living at the church hostel with a few other destitute women. She learnt tailoring and embroidery in a training school run by a local NGO, which ran the shop for her and helped her maintain the accounts. She not only made new stylish clothes at affordable prices but also altered and mended old clothes.

Seeing Lakshmi walking up to her shop, Keka ran out and hugged her. 'Come in, Lakshmi di. Have some tea,' Keka said softly. She then showed Lakshmi around her shop and asked her if she wanted to get something tailored.

'Keka, I'm very happy that you're getting to do this. But I need your help,' Lakshmi said.

Keka was expecting a sad, disappointed Lakshmi but instead she sounded determined.

'So many rich girls from Noor Manzil get their dresses stitched from you. They have high-class clients. Can you introduce me to them? I need an entry…'

Keka had not expected this. They had met each other a few times since Keka had got out of the home. And they had discussed the film and the award and all the interviews that Lakshmi had given to journalists. Keka had seen Lakshmi go from being hopeful to dejected. But this was a different Lakshmi and Keka was shocked at this sudden change. 'Are you sure this is what you want to do?' Keka asked.

'I'm beyond help now, Keka. The angels in my life were temporary visitors. They've forgotten me and I need to forget them and the shiny life they tempted me with.'

'Didi, why don't you talk to Father Julius…or Prateek. I'm sure they can find some way to help—'

'No, Keka. I'm tired of being at the mercy of men. If I've learnt anything from my education, it is self-reliance. My grandmother was a prostitute and my mother is a practising one. It runs in my blood...I cannot escape it, but I can turn it to my advantage. You are lucky that you escaped this fate. Yes, you missed going to England, but your life is better than mine,' Lakshmi's voice was harsh and she almost sounded like her mother.

Keka sat down beside Lakshmi and took her hands in hers.

'But I don't want to live and work like the girls here. I need to lead a cleaner and healthier life, like...like the girls of Noor Manzil and Prem Manzil. Many such girls are your customers. Can you introduce me to them?' Lakshmi asked again.

Keka promised to help her. Lakshmi was determined and Keka had the means to help her. But as it turned out, fate took a hand and brought Lakshmi a better solution. Hers would not be just another Sonagachi story.

BOOK III

11.

Lakshmi was crossing Chittaranjan Avenue when a shiny black car came hurtling round the corner. It veered to avoid her and she jumped back and cursed.

The young man who was driving the car braked hard, rolled the window down and yelled out his apologies.

'Don't you have eyes?' Lakshmi screamed at him in English.

'I jumped a red light and brushed against a traffic constable's bike. He's after me. Help me. I need to hide. My licence has been punched twice already.'

Lakshmi made a split-second decision. She jumped into the car and guided the driver into the lanes of Sonagachi. Though the streets were relatively empty at that time, the young man found himself negotiating people, dogs, cattle, van rickshaws and suchlike in the narrow lanes. Once they reached her house, Lakshmi asked him to pull over.

'That was close!' he sighed. 'I don't think he'll be able to follow me in here. What a maze this is! I'll wait here for some time to make sure that no one has followed me. But you have to help me get out of here…please…'

Now that they were in her area and her heart had stopped pounding, Lakshmi examined the young man next to her. He was slightly built, but good-looking and well dressed. She didn't know much about cars, but this looked like an expensive one. The seats and interior were plush and the AC was blasting, making it so comfortable that Lakshmi didn't want to go back into the heat. A yellow ambassador taxi was the best car she had experienced so far.

'Now, give me a thousand rupees!' demanded Lakshmi.

'What? Even the constable would not have asked for more than two hundred rupees!'

'But he would have taken your licence! And maybe your car as well.'

'Yes... That's true,' he said. 'And my card has got punched twice already.'

'So, a thousand rupees isn't too much, no? If you don't have the cash now, you can drive me to the nearest ATM. It's just five minutes away.'

'I've never seen a girl asking for money so shamelessly...' He broke off, having noticed the women standing around. 'Is this a brothel?' he asked

'Such an innocent! Don't you know this is Sonagachi?'

The young man was shocked into silence. Lakshmi laughed at his discomfiture.

'You live here?' he finally asked.

'I practise sex,' Lakshmi said. This was something that she had heard the volunteers at the NGO say.

'No way. Don't joke. You look out of place here. There must be a story. Can we have coffee somewhere?'

Lakshmi looked at him carefully. Could he be a fraud? Going outside Sonagachi with a stranger was risky, after all. But this could be a chance for her to make some quick money. He looked rich but young and decent enough, she concluded. He didn't look down upon her and spoke to her like an equal, something that the rich brats who came to Sonagachi didn't do. They spoke rudely, used choicest slangs while addressing the girls. The girls had to put up with their nonsense only because they had money.

'Okay, I can go out with you for some time. But money first. Or we know how to raise hell,' she said raising her voice.

'Okay, okay. There's no need to shout. I still can't believe you're from here and you do what you said you do. Where do you live?'

Lakshmi pointed to her shack. The man looked at the dark and dirty entrance to the ground floor rooms and then again looked at her with disbelief. Lakshmi laughed. She was enjoying herself.

'I'm Rahul,' he gave her his hand.

Lakshmi took it, 'My name is Lakshmi.'

He drove them to a coffee shop on Park Street. The evening rush hour traffic hadn't begun and they were at the outlet in about twenty minutes, before Lakshmi could complain about how far he was taking her. She was wearing a clean and fresh salwar kameez and hadn't put on her work make-up. She didn't look too out of place. She tried to be nonchalant, like she frequented high-end cafés all the time. But when she looked at the menu, she found she didn't understand anything. What were these? So many types of coffee? So, when Rahul asked her what she wanted, she smiled sweetly and told him to order the same thing he was getting.

After the steaming cups were served, Rahul turned to Lakshmi. Rahul had also ordered sandwiches and when these arrived with the coffee, she felt her stomach growl and she began to salivate.

'Now tell me your story. I promise I'll pay you.'

'There's no story. I'm a prostitute. I live and work in Sonagachi.'

'So how do you speak such good English?'

'For a while I went to school and was tutored by a foreign couple,' she said dismissively. She didn't want to tell this stranger about her life.

'I'm a DJ in a night club around here. This is Park Street,' Rahul said.

'Park Street, the place where the city parties, isn't it? You work around here? Great! Can you find me something to do? I know call girls are in great demand here…' Lakshmi said.

'Look, I know some people who want girls to party with. Girls who they can have fun with, of course, for a price. Will you come? They're rich, you'll make good money. I'll help to set you up, and you give me my commission.'

'But how will I be able to move with rich people? I don't have the right clothes…you know where I am from.'

'Don't worry about that. I'll help you. Do you have a contact number?'

'No.'

'Take mine. Call me tomorrow at 2 p.m. Now take your money.' Rahul handed her two five hundred-rupee notes and saw her eyes brighten. He wasn't a fraud after all.

By the time Lakshmi called Rahul the next day, he had fixed up her first client—a college boy, the son of a millionaire. He had planned a party at the family's guest house on Loudon Street. Rahul picked Lakshmi up from the entrance of Sovabazar Metro Station at the appointed time and drove straight to his flat.

'This area is Jodhpur Park. Have you ever come this side?'

'No,' Lakshmi said, craning her neck to look at the houses

and apartments in the locality. 'Do you live alone?' she asked as they walked into his well-appointed flat.

'Yes. I had a roommate, but he's moved to Mumbai.'

'Your parents?'

'They live in Howrah. They don't approve of my profession. And once they found out I was gay, they threw me out.' He stopped to see if she understood what 'gay' meant. He could see that she didn't, so he explained.

'I have sex only with men. Homosexual…gay…you understand? So you're safe with me!' he laughed.

Lakshmi was shocked. She knew of the men who came looking for young boys in Sonagachi, but it was always considered a perversion, something to whisper about and hide. Rahul didn't seem to be ashamed though and was comfortable with his sexuality.

'Don't be surprised. These days we prefer to live openly. You will find many people like me in these party circles if you decide to work with me.'

But there was no time to chat. They had to get ready for the party. Rahul had bought a few pairs of jeans and some tops.

'I had to guess your size, I hope something fits you. Keep them in any case and use them until you can buy your own clothes. Pay me back when you have money. I'll keep the accounts.'

Lakshmi examined the clothes. They were bright, colourful and well made. 'Thank you, I think they will fit nicely,' Lakshmi said, smiling.

'Go to the washroom, freshen up and then try these on. I also got some make-up and perfume for you. Keep your make-up light and fresh. You're going to a big party tonight.'

Lakshmi wore the jeans and a cherry red top, did her make-up and walked out.

'Wow! You look smashing…'

Lakshmi knew she looked good. But she was nervous. 'Rahul, I've taken a great risk coming with you. Please don't abandon me,' Lakshmi looked earnestly at him.

'I'll introduce you, but I won't hang around. I'll come back on time and make sure you get back home. Never show how nervous you are. Also, you need a new name. Lakshmi is too old-fashioned. How do you like the name Anjali?' he went on, not giving her time to react.

'There will be about eight or ten people at the party—boys and girls. They will be smoking, drinking and at some stage, they'll do drugs. You don't need to do the drugs, but it will help if you look like you're drinking, but make sure you don't get drunk. Do you dance? The Bollywood-type gyrations, I mean, nothing serious. Be friendly with everyone and pay attention to each one's demands, but tonight your date is Shekhar. It's his party. Okay?'

Lakshmi nodded.

'Try to have fun, Anjali. You are starting out on a new journey and this could be a game changer for you,' Rahul said cheerily as he linked his arm through hers and led her off. Lakshmi's heart pounded hard. She put on a confident smile and hoped no one could see how scared she really felt.

◆

The party was getting a bit rowdy, and loud. Rahul had introduced her to the group and left to DJ at a club nearby. Most of the people were roaring drunk and the drugs had come out. She felt a little worried, but it was a young fun group of people who were friendly and tried to make her feel comfortable. Shekhar, her date, had been talking to her for a while now. He would excuse himself every now and then and make sure that the rest of his guests were doing okay. She realized how young they were. She was the same age as them, but their lives were so different, so carefree and in a way, so innocent. They were happily spending their parents' money. She felt a little lost—she had so much to learn.

But later at night when Shekhar took her into the bedroom and closed the door, she realized that she would have to be the teacher. Shekhar said he had been with girls before, but it was clear that he was a novice. He was awkward and clumsy. She guided him step by step, all the while making him feel like he was leading. The combination of alcohol and his inexperience meant that he finished almost as soon as he started. Lakshmi made the appropriate noises and gave the young man the encouragement he needed. Then they cuddled for a while and soon Shekhar drifted off to sleep. Lakshmi went to the attached bathroom and cleaned up. Shekhar was still asleep when she came out, so she decided to go out and see what was happening.

One couple was passed out on the sofa, entwined with each other, one of the boys was asleep on the carpet, an empty bottle of whisky lying next to him. The other bedrooms were closed. She went into the kitchen and found the food that had been left in the takeout boxes. It was all untouched. The biryani and chicken kebabs smelled wonderful and she was hungry. She helped herself.

Rahul turned up on time as agreed. He got the money from Shekhar and gave Lakshmi her share. Fifteen thousand rupees for an evening of partying with fun, young people didn't seem like a bad deal to her. Rahul kept five thousand for himself, and to

Lakshmi that seemed perfectly fair. Shekhar said bye to her with a long kiss. He wanted to see her again.

That was just the beginning. Rahul kept her busy most weekends. He even arranged for Lakshmi to use his flat when her rich clients didn't have anywhere to take her. Not all the parties were like the first one she went to. There were designer drug parties, rave parties, swap parties and multiple-partner parties. Lakshmi found her way around all of these. There had been a few hiccups, but she was quick to learn and didn't make the same mistake twice. The same rules she had learnt from Suhani stood her in good stead. Rich or poor, men were men, she decided.

◆

Once Lakshmi started seeing regular work with Rahul's friends and clients, she stopped taking on customers in her room. But she made sure that she handed over the agreed amount to her mother every week. But Malati was not satisfied with this. As always, she worried about losing her grip on her daughter.

'Where were you all night, Lakshmi?' Malati said as Lakshmi was unlocking the door to her room at the crack of dawn. Her mother had been sitting on the steps and waiting. Her voice was cold with anger.

'Why are you here?' Lakshmi asked.

'Answer the question.'

'Stop shouting at me,' Lakshmi was in no mood to let her mother bully her.

'You've not become such a big person that I won't hit you. Started earning two paisa and already challenging me? How dare you! I'm not only your mother, but your owner too. You owe me an explanation for your movements outside Sonagachi,' Malati yelled.

'You are NOT my owner. No one can own me,' Lakshmi hissed.

'I'll lock you in here. Then let's see where you go.'

'Lock me up here, and you'll starve,' Lakshmi said. She took out a few notes from her handbag and threw them at her mother. Malati stared daggers at her daughter. Lakshmi ignored her and walked in, feeling victorious. Malati hurriedly picked up the notes and walked away.

Lakshmi had mostly been seen as an obedient and docile girl. In fact, Malati sometimes wondered how the girl had turned out to be so timid unlike her. She was happy that the girl stood out in Sonagachi because of her brush with the foreigners. It had increased her price manifold, but as she had feared, Lakshmi's aspirations changed. Malati could no longer keep close tabs on her. And she couldn't put any more pressure on Lakshmi since she had her own customers and earned good money without her mother's involvement.

Lakshmi had managed to climb out of the squalor of Sonagachi as far as her clients were concerned. But she still didn't have the courage to look for quarters outside Sonagachi. She had to come back to her room and to her mother who was growing more distrustful every day. She needed to do more: to bid goodbye to Sonagachi and wrest control of her income from Rahul. But this required patience and planning. And Lakshmi…Anjali, as she was learning to think of herself, was going to get out.

12.

The heat was stifling. The fan was on at full speed, vibrating noisily, but all it did was beat down hot air. Anjali could not go back to sleep. Her night gown was drenched. She got out of bed, and walked over to the window and pushed it open. A cool gust hit her face and she took a deep breath. This small two-bedroom flat in Sovabazar was a far cry from her hovel in Sonagachi, but it was just a stepping stone. She looked around her in the gloomy light and felt a surge of pride for how far she had come. If any of her clients ever saw her modest house in this middle-class neighbourhood, they would turn their nose up at it and she would lose their business. But, of course, she never brought any of her customers here. While the usual Sonagachi client would think of this flat as plush, she had stopped servicing such men.

When she had first started working with Rahul, he had warned her to never let anyone know where she really lived. 'Don't tell anyone ever.' Even Rahul had never deigned to step into her small room in Sonagachi. 'You are my roommate. This is where you live,' he had said, referring to his flat.

Even without his warning, Anjali knew she could never let anyone know where she came from. The story Rahul had put about in the beginning was that Anjali had left home because she didn't get along with her parents which is why she worked as an escort to make a living. No one questioned this. Anjali learned to fit in with the rich crowd.

But Rahul was no longer a huge part of her life. A few years after she met him, Anjali found out about the places that rich businessmen frequented. She made contacts easily and managed to set up her own clients. As she explored, she found that she particularly liked The Owl—a popular night club on Park Street attached to a five-star hotel. She had learnt to look the part of a successful executive. Her clothes fit her well, her make-up was subtle and well applied and her accessories looked expensive. She looked like she belonged. The clients here were definitely not young students—they were successful executives and businessmen. Some of them were locals and others were visiting the city on work. And some among them were looking for company for a night or two. It was here that she met the suave Sohail Khan. He was a successful businessman who was on the boards of several companies.

'I didn't expect to meet such a finished product,' he'd said the first time they met. They had been introduced through another client of Anjali's. Sohail's wife and son lived in the US while he worked in Kolkata. He was in his sixties, but was well groomed, fit and could pass for ten years younger. He liked going to the best restaurants and appreciated good food and enjoyed her young, pretty company. He introduced her to his associates and clients. As she began spending time with this crowd, Anjali realized that the flirting and joking she had been doing with the younger lot would not work. These men were older, more experienced. They wanted to have their fun in bed, but would expect her to be able to hold her own in a smart conversation. They were willing to pay a price for the experience. Though they came to her for fun, relaxation and sex, she needed to understand more about their worlds and worries. Suhani had taught her to always get the measure of the man she was with. So Anjali started reading newspapers, especially the business pages. She mentally thanked Zoya aunty for having given her the foundations on which she was building her life. This was not the life they had planned together, but that dream had long since dissipated. Instead of getting a degree, Anjali gained a different sort of knowledge. Sohail encouraged her to go to finishing school. It gave her the edge she needed—sometimes she was in competition with college girls. With the sophistication that she learnt and her own smarts, Anjali was able to taste steady success. She knew how to hold her end of a conversation and learnt to subtly massage the egos of powerful men. Soon she started getting regular assignments. She cast off Lakshmi's crude Sonagachi skin and fully remade herself as the suave Anjali.

◆

Anjali had spent the night with Sohail. Room service had just brought up breakfast. She poured out coffee for both of them. Sohail put down the paper and turned to her.

She turned to smile at him, but then realized that he had a serious expression on his face.

'What's the matter?' she asked him, alarmed that she had said or done something that he was angry about.

'How would you like to meet the great Anant Agarwal?' he asked her.

Anant Agarwal was a very successful businessman who had

made his name and money in real estate. He had developed properties all over India and the Middle East. Over the years, he had diversified into the hospitality, education, health and entertainment sectors. Anjali had heard of him, even seen him at some gatherings. He was a forbidding man. Over six feet tall, with a deep throaty voice, he was a handsome man who always looked solemn. At every party that Anjali had seen him, Anant was the centre of attention. Anjali realized that this was not only because of his wealth. There was something mesmeric about him. Anjali had wondered if he would ever notice her. But he ignored all the beautiful, well-accomplished women around him, what chance did she stand? He was courteous, but aloof.

'He's looking for a…companion,' Sohail said. 'And I suggested that you might be the right person.'

She smiled. 'Of course, I'd love to meet him. But he's always surrounded by the most beautiful women. Why would he want my company?'

'Leave that to me. He wants you to go with him to China.'

'That's a long way to go for a date,' she laughed.

'It's not a date, think of it more as an audition. Your life could change,' said Sohail. 'And take it seriously. I'm taking it seriously as well. If Anant likes you, he won't want to share you with me. I'm willing to let you go. Do you understand why I would do that?'

She understood. He was trading her. Clearly, Sohail saw some advantage in that. For a second, she felt disappointment. How easily he passed her on. But she knew how this world turned. Perhaps this would prove to be an advantage for her as well.

Anjali and Anant had their first date at one of his properties. It was a huge commercial complex with offices. The top floor had serviced apartments and guest houses. Sohail told her that Anant wanted them to meet before making arrangements for the trip to China.

Anjali knew she had to make an impression. Rather than her usual tailored western suits, she decided to wear a sari—a beautiful Bengal cotton in red and white. She knew there was a risk that she would be seen as 'middle-class'—something that could spell the end of one's social climbing. But she knew that by doing something unexpected, she would stand out.

They had a leisurely drink together, then Anant asked for the dinner to be brought in. As they ate, he told her a little bit about his business and the travel that it entailed. He asked her about her life and family. Anjali made the decision on the spot—she told him the truth. It was a risk, but one that paid off. Anant was interested in her and seemed to admire her for coming so far.

She couldn't read him, though—clearly it would take more than one evening to get to know him. But Anant made up his mind and asked her to accompany him on the China trip.

'May I ask you something?' Anjali replied.

He nodded.

'You could have anyone or anything you want. So why did you ask for me?'

'I've heard good things from Sohail about your intelligence and discretion. And I've noticed you at parties. I can tell you have what it takes—the right combination of business sense and sensuality. So, China?'

Anjali was delighted to agree.

Anjali had accompanied some of her customers to Bali and Mauritius. China was a very different sort of place. She didn't get to see too much of it and they were accompanied everywhere.

The only time she and Anant had time together was once he got back to the hotel. They had gotten along rather well. Anjali could see that he was serious in public and during business meetings, but he enjoyed the lightness that she brought into his world. He didn't laugh easily, but when she pulled his leg or made an incisive remark, his eyes twinkled. She turned it into a game for herself—trying to get him to smile.

After two weeks, Anjali came back to Kolkata on her own as Anant carried on to Europe. But he had arranged for a car to drop her home from the airport. When the shiny limousine drew up, Anjali shuddered at the thought of taking the car into the narrow lanes of her neighbourhood. She tried to tell the driver to let her out at the end of the main road. But he insisted on driving her to the gate and opening the door for her.

A few days after she came back from China, she got a call from Prateek. They had kept in touch, but Anjali largely avoided these conversations. All his work at the NGO had only made Prateek more rigid about sex work. He disapproved of her choices—he could see that she now had expensive clothes and shoes and bags. He hated to think about how she was earning all this. He repeatedly tried to convince her to do something else. This conversation was no different.

'Lakshmi, I have an exciting job offer,' he started. 'The NGO is looking for someone to coordinate with all the offices in the country. They need someone smart who can speak English. You will need some training and I can help you with that. Why don't you apply? They're offering a monthly salary of twenty thousand rupees. I might be able to negotiate for a little more.'

Anjali realized with sadness how far apart they had grown. Did he really think that was a big amount? Her world had become so much larger. She had seen real money and there was no way she would go back to her old life.

'Prateek, I'm busy now, I'll talk to you later,' she had hung up before they got into another argument.

Anjali had to wait until Anant came back from his Europe trip before she could find out how she had performed in the audition. Their next date was at the same guest house. The long separation seemed to have increased Anant's appetite for her. As soon as she stepped in, he drew her to himself roughly and tore off her clothes. He was impatient, almost rough with her. Once he had spent himself, he was calmer. And was ready to talk about what he wanted from her.

Anjali had been a little anxious. Sohail had been sure that he would ask her to make their arrangement exclusive. But Anant had bigger plans than she had envisioned.

'I need someone to handle all my clients' entertainment,' he said to her. He had hinted as much in China, so this was not a surprise. 'Drop all your other clients,' he said in his brusque way. 'I know you support your mother and of course you should continue doing that. But drop your old friends and acquaintances. I'll set you up in your own home. But you have to make yourself available to me and only to me. This will be an exclusive association. You'll need to organize certain events, entertain at these parties… Some of my associates will also want you to organize escorts for them. Can you handle this?'

Anjali was thrilled but nervous. There was a very big opportunity here and if she played her cards right, she could… Anjali couldn't even imagine all the ways in which her life could change. But she was a shrewd woman and had learnt more than seduction and party planning from her time with the powerful.

She had learnt the art of negotiation and was aware of her own worth. She negotiated the terms, making sure that she got what she wanted. Apart from the house, servants and a car and driver for her use, she demanded a monthly allowance to spend on herself. She would also earn from the commissions she made on arranging escorts.

She agreed enthusiastically. Anant was happy to get what he wanted. He pulled her to him. For the first time ever, Anjali returned his embrace with real, genuine enthusiasm.

◆

'Nest' is what Anjali started calling her new home. That was not the name on the board outside, but that is how she thought of it. It was a sprawling flat in the posh Salt Lake area. Anant had left some furniture and artwork there already, but gave Anjali an allowance to decorate the way she wanted. As she walked around her new home, she thought back to her first home with her grandmother and mother. The small pooja space, the bed in the corner of the room, the dark walls, the constant noise from all the neighbouring houses squashed together. It seemed so distant… almost like a bad dream! What was her mother doing at this very moment, she wondered. She must be cooking for herself and Paltu uncle. Her heart went out to them. Anjali was diligent about sending her mother money every week. Malati no longer had to work. But she was clear that her mother should never be able to find her. She had not told Malati anything yet. She planned to call her later in the day and let her know that she no longer lived in her old Sovabazar flat. She had informed Prateek that she was moving away, but she refused to tell him where she was going.

For the first few months, Anjali was very careful, she didn't want to take a single false step. She was in awe of Anant and nervous about making him happy. She knew that she could satiate him sexually, but it was the other work—planning parties, organizing girls for his business associates—that she was nervous about.

Anant had been transparent about the nature of their arrangement. He had told Anjali that he would provide for all her needs but she should not consider herself his girlfriend or mistress. There would be no emotional strings—she had no right to demand anything or even expect anything from him. This was not really onerous. Anant was a private person and slow to open up about himself. But slowly, he came to depend on her for emotional support. He told her about his marriage. It was the same old story. His wife was from a big industrial family and their marriage had been arranged by their parents. They had nothing in common and the marriage was in name only. She ran a fashion label and had her own social circle. They kept their marriage going since it was convenient for both of them but they led separate lives.

Anant introduced Anjali to the larger group around him as his personal assistant. But whispers followed her—enough people knew that she was an escort. Word got around. But they didn't dare say anything to Anjali—they did not want to draw Anant's ire. But there was a lot of attention on Anjali and she had to learn to deflect it. She sensed the jealousy over her looks and popularity, but she also knew that many of them thought of her as inferior. This was a battle Anjali fought with herself as well. These were rich, educated women who were accomplished in their own fields. Those who did not work at jobs were involved in charity work and cultural organizations. She couldn't hope to compete with them. But she didn't need to. She had to make sure that she did what Anant demanded of her. And where her role in Anant's life was concerned, she held her own.

She worked day and night to win Anant's trust because she knew, as her mother had known, that her beauty and body would please him only for a few years. Inevitably, someone younger and more appealing would come along. Anjali wanted to make sure that even when she was no longer Anant's sexual partner, she still had a job. She became the key entertainer for his top clients, even bought his clothes and shoes, kept track of his personal diary. She came to know him a lot better and learnt to anticipate him. She managed to delight him with her forethought and they became a formidable team. Anant came to think of her as a permanent part of his life. But even in her thoughts, she didn't dare to label their relationship.

Epilogue

Anjali and I sat opposite each other, sipping our tea and looking out of the window of her first floor living room. It had been six years since my first stress-filled trip to meet her. Over the years, we had kept in touch and she had told me a lot about her life. But the past few times she had called, asking if I would join her for lunch or tea, I hadn't been able to get away from work and personal commitments to visit. So after finishing an assignment not too far from her house, I had called to find out if I could drop in. It was a weekday morning—she was usually free then. Anjali was only too happy to see me.

'Anjali! I'm so glad you were free to see me, dear.'

'Don't joke, I'm always free to see you. You've not been here in so long. The busy journalist that you are!' she said in mock anger.

'I am so sorry, Anjali, but you're never far from my mind. You know that!'

She wore a simple off-white top and a blue wrap-around skirt. She was looking relaxed, her skin was glowing. Her thick shiny hair had been scrunched into an untidy bun; she wore a thin gold chain around her neck, a gold bracelet on her right wrist and a gold watch on the left. She looked almost ethereal and I couldn't take my eyes off her. She was not young anymore, but the years sat well on her and added to her grace and poise.

Her maid had left us tea and cookies on a tray. We picked up our cups and settled down to chat. The conversation veered from my assignments and how newspapers across the country were not doing well to job cuts and general insecurities all around. Anjali's analysis of the political scenario in the state was that the ruling party was gradually losing its goodwill with the elite, though its rural base remained intact.

'Call an election tomorrow and you will be surprised at the resounding victory that the chief minister will manage to pull off. But that definitely doesn't reflect the state of affairs of the state,' she said, gesturing at the newspapers that lay on the divan. I agreed with her analysis. 'You've been following current affairs quite closely!' I said, not surprised.

'Yes, Anant is very close to the powerful. That means I get close to them as well. A bit of reflected glory, if you will…' Anjali laughed. She then gave me driblets of gossip from Anant's business world. Each of them could have become stories in the finance section or the gossip columns. But Anjali knew I wouldn't spill. I had kept all her secrets so far. I was one of the few people whom she was comfortable around. The rest of her circle either wanted something from her or would love to bring her down. In her own way, she was a powerful woman, setting up meetings, inviting the who's who, helping form liaisons, quelling misunderstandings and forging ties…all in the background. The powerful always have enemies and Anjali was no exception.

Although she had told me about her grandmother and her mother, her personal life is not a topic Anjali brought up often. But every now and then, she would confide in me when something was troubling her. These were problems that I couldn't give her solutions to, but all she wanted was for me to listen. She had many admirers, but hardly anyone to talk to. That must be very lonely. Today, she seemed to be thinking about one of her old lovers. She had mentioned him to me earlier, but only to say it ended badly.

'Remember I told you about Rajiv all those years ago?' she said out of the blue. She had told me that he had proposed marriage to her but it had not worked out.

I nodded. 'So what happened? Did he change his mind?' I asked her.

'No, Rajiv was genuine. But he was troubled. All he wanted to do was escape his life and loveless marriage. I had met him before I met Anant. Then he got married and I didn't see him for a few years. He came back into my life soon after I moved in here. It was a confusing time. The first few years here were hard. Not everyone in Anant's circle accepted me. I was worried that I would trip up and someone would only be too glad to make sure I was out of here. So, when Rajiv came back, it felt familiar, he was supportive, I thought I was in love. He told me the same old story about his wife not satisfying him. He wanted to leave her. When he proposed I was so happy, but, really, I was young and stupid. What would Rajiv's family have done if they came to know he was divorcing his wife for a prostitute? He worked in the family business, after all. And while he made sweet promises, would he have really divorced his wife and married me? And Anant? He has a temper… He's always been good to me, but he does think he has a right over me. I shudder to think what he would have done.

'So the next time we met, I tried to discuss this with Rajiv but he wouldn't listen. He was floating away on this dream. He desperately wanted to start a family with me. He became rather obsessed. And I started to think, what was the point of getting away from my mother if all I was going to do was give control of my life to this man?

'Okay, maybe he might have calmed down once we were married but Rajiv desperately wanted a family. I began to question what kind of mother I would make. I come from a line of sex workers. What would I tell my children about where they come from?

'Can you imagine what it would do to a child to find out… I can't imagine doing that to an innocent child. I called Rajiv and told him that I didn't love him. That I was just having fun with him.'

'And he believed you?'

'I don't know. But he wouldn't let me go so easily. He threatened to tell Anant. That's when I realized how much this arrangement with Anant meant. How hard I had worked to get here, all the dreams I had sacrificed. I got scared, I knew that Rajiv didn't know his limits and didn't care about the consequences of his actions. I decided to get in front of it. I told Anant a version of the story and begged for forgiveness…and promised never to stray again… I'm lucky, he forgave me.'

'Did you love him, Rajiv, I mean?' I asked her.

'When you become so very good at faking love, real love tends to become elusive. Was Rajiv really the love of my life? I can't say,' Anjali said.

'So you don't have any regrets?' I asked her.

'Honestly, no. I had the choice to leave, but I wanted security. I never wanted to go back and live like my mother and grandmother.'

'Are you in touch with your mother?' I asked.

'Not in a regular sort of way. I mean, I don't visit her, but I send her money. She doesn't work anymore and has let out her rooms to another woman. Prateek has helped her and Paltu uncle find a small apartment near Sovabazar. I want them to live in peace now and leave me in peace. She doesn't have my number, has no idea where I live.' Anjali sighed.

'I've always wondered why you haven't kept in touch with Prateek more. He's so genuine and dependable,' I asked.

'Yes, he is. And he won't stop judging me for my choices. He's never liked my ambitious streak. What do we have in common in any case? Our mothers? I think we would both like to leave that part of our past behind.'

She was right, I realized. Prateek wanted to rescue her. I had spoken to him again after that meeting when he finally put me in touch with Anjali. He had tried to convince me to talk to her about changing her life. But she had made her peace with the direction her life had gone and the difficult choices she'd had to make. Prateek didn't understand that.

'Thank you for listening to me,' Anjali reached over and held my hand. 'I don't have anyone in my life that I can talk to about these things. I go to spas, gyms, meditation and yoga classes. But some days, I feel a heaviness.' She trailed off and smiled at me. I squeezed her hand.

'It feels like it might rain,' she said, gathering herself and turning to look out of the window.

We both fell silent as the evening came on and lights began twinkling in the distance.

Acknowledgements

I have lived with this book for so long that it has ceased to be a story and has turned into some kind of an alternate reality. It all started, just as you have read in the Prologue, with *Slumdog Millionaire* winning at the Oscars. I went back to Sonagachi to trace the little heroes of the award-winning documentary *Born Into Brothels* and the seeds of the novel were sown. A usual newspaper story of 500 words was published the next day and Sajal Mukherjee was the photographer who had accompanied me. We got talking about how this article had the makings of a novel.

A journalist's life is hectic, you live and die every day, but in the midst of this hectic activity, the story started bothering me and got me to put pen to paper. Though based on a true encounter, *Not Just Another Story* is a work of fiction. Through the course of twenty-five years of journalism, I have often gone back to Sonagachi to do several stories on rare achievements, diseases, deaths, exploitation...and every time I have come back with a new realization. I have tried to bring in some of that in this novel.

After having written my story, I didn't know which publisher I should approach, and wrote to Shashi Tharoor, whose book I had just translated into Bengali. He liked the first two chapters and forwarded these with a note to David Davidar. That set the ball rolling.

I am happy that Mr Davidar assigned the editing to Pujitha Krishnan with whom I have travelled this very unique and what at times seemed like a never-ending journey. But finally we arrived.

I thank the *Times of India* for giving me endless opportunities daily to stumble upon stories that often end up being life-changing experiences.

I'd like to thank my father, who is no more, for believing in me when the rest of the world thought I was daydreaming. He believed that unless you let your mind laze, it doesn't wander and if it doesn't wander, it doesn't imagine! I thank my mother for never being content with my achievements…her way of pushing me to do better. I thank my husband for bearing with me as I spent my time in this fictional world. I thank my son for calling me 'creative' even when he thought the word meant naughty. They have all, in their unique ways, helped to kindle the flame.